A DRINK OF THE Devils WINE

DANIEL LEE SILVERTHORNE

ISBN-10: 0578119609
EAN-13: 9780578119601

Library of Congress Control Number: 2013904446
CreateSpace Independent Publishing Platform
North Charleston, South Carolina

Dedication

To my wife, my mom, and my Aunt Julie.
The three strongest and most influential people in my life

Acknowledgments

I'd like to offer my thanks to Sean Shinners, Brandon Lucas, Beth Milstead Claeys, and professor Susan Mowers for their continual support and valuable feedback.

Contents

"it ain't nothing a little killing won't fix..."

Ron "Little Chief" Wantlan

Introduction

It was one of those nights where nothing was going to happen and no one was going to bother me, and that was just the way I preferred it. I was becoming less of a drinker as I got older, but now and then a good bourbon or scotch would grab my attention and tonight was my time to chill. I had grabbed a booth in the back corner of Tillman's lounge; I always picked a seat with a clear view of the room and my back to a wall. What can I say, old habits die hard, and the fact that I was still alive was testament to the fact that in spite of my other downfalls in life I was still very good at my job. Tillman's was an old school steak joint where a lot of business and whispered deals had gone down, along with a lot of steaks and booze. The food was simple and good. The drinks were strong, and it was one of the few places left where you wouldn't have some 21 year old bimbo incessantly bothering you, while doing a poor impression of a waitress, asking to many questions, and smiling way too much. The walls were crushed velvet, and matched just fine with the crimson carpet, black leather seats, and the ever present faint aroma of old cigar smoke. Smoking in restaurants had long ago been outlawed, but sometimes history just won't die. It wasn't the kind of place you'd take a date, and half the patrons looked like they had one foot in the grave and another on a banana peel, but for what I needed tonight it was perfect. I had a short tumbler of Glenfiddich sitting in front of me, the two ice cubes and the lemon twist just starting to introduce each other, when the vaguely familiar face approached. I knew that I had met the sharp dressed old man somewhere in the past, but I couldn't remember from where. Apparently he noticed this and said it's been a long time and I didn't expect you to remember me, can I join you? I was just beginning to let myself fade into the ambience of the place, and really did not want company or conversation, and I don't know if it was respect for my elders or not wanting to offend the old man, but I said sure, sit down.

I had ordered a New York strip, bloody rare, fries, and a Caesar salad, and as the waitress came with my salad and some rolls I asked the old guy if he was hungry or wanted a drink. He said no to food, but yes to a snifter of the house brandy. I asked the waitress to make it the good stuff, and as quickly as she disappeared she reappeared, drink in hand. The old guy thanked her, and then me, and I said you're welcome, now no offense, but where do I know you from and what is it you want. He said his name was Sam and we had some of the same friends a long time ago. I guessed him to be in his 60s from appearance, but in truth his actual age was deep into the 70s, and he didn't look to be slowing down any time soon. He maintained a steel gaze throughout our conversation, with a handshake to match, and in spite of his relaxed manner, like me he was aware of everything that was happening anywhere in the room. I had no doubt in my mind that if one of the regulars sitting at the bar had decided to test their luck, youth, or manhood with Sam, they would have suffered a very bad night. I let his comment sink in as I chewed a mouthful of lettuce. Damn it was nice to still be able to find a place that knew how to make a Caesar salad, none of that fake processed liquid that came out of a jar, and a bunch of toppings that didn't belong there. Just chopped romaine, dressing made from scratch, a few croutons, and some fresh grated parmesan, and not the crap that came out of a cardboard jar either. I washed it down with a satisfied sip of my scotch, leaned slightly back in the booth and said okay.

Sam looked at me for a moment, pausing to gather his next statement, and said I don't really want anything, other than maybe another pros perspective on what we do, and the life we chose. Typically I would have simply given his comment an unrevealing silence, this wasn't a business that involved much shop talk, but for some reason, maybe it was gut instinct alone, I had a small amount of trust in my new acquaintance. Still I didn't reply, just yet. He said I've done a lot of work in my day, and this isn't confession, I'm not dying, and I'm not under a wire from the cops, but I guess I just have human curiosity. I have pretty much retired, and now I find myself pondering many issues of why after the sun goes down. You're younger than me so I assume these issues have yet to perplex you, or affect a good night's sleep, and don't get me wrong he said, I'm not worried about missing the bus to heaven either, truth is I never really thought I had a chance well before any of this. I did my first killing out of anger, pure and simple, but like many of us someone noticed I had the aptitude and ability, and my recruitment wasn't long after. The waitress appeared, clearing my plate, offering a refill, which we both accepted, and disappearing once more. Our conversation had temporarily stopped, which gave me time to chew on what I'd just heard, but I wasn't yet ready to engage, so the old man went on. I heard you had some rules to what jobs you accepted, I never did. For me it was always business, and business was always welcome as long as the money was right, after all I had retirement to consider. He paused, took another sip of his brandy, and looked at me with a slight grin. I'm not sure if he was trying to gain my trust, thought it was a good night for telling your life story, or maybe really was under the wire, so I tested him. You said we had some of the same friends back in the day, who and when?

He went on to describe some associations and history that started to give him a little credibility, but just a little. I challenged some of his statements, digging a little deeper into his proposed link to me, and every time he came back with the right answer, still I wasn't going to lay out my resume and work history, no matter how convincing he might be. The second round of drinks arrived, along with my steak, still sizzling on the plate. You sure you're not hungry I said. I'm sure he said the brandy is doing me just fine. I let my steak rest on the plate. You didn't want to screw up such a gorgeous hunk of meat with impatience, and as the rich smell filled the air I thought to take another drink, but I didn't. From an outsiders perspective this conversation might have appeared humorous, but the topic of conversation right now did not allow the luxury of humor, or being taken lightly. Jesus I thought, for a night that was supposed to be relaxing this is turning into a lot of damn work. Still the situation was increasingly arousing my curiosity, and maybe that's the real reason why I hadn't stopped it 20 minutes ago.

So what was your first job, I asked. It wasn't a job he replied, like I said it was just the result of the anger of a young man. My mom was raising me and my brother and sister, living in a two bit piece of shit apartment in Cleveland, cleaning houses for whatever the rich folks felt like paying, and all of us barely hanging on. My mom had this derelict man friend named Frank that I never liked. My dad had died when I was a baby and I guess she just needed some occasional companionship, regardless of how disgusting it might be. He used to come over late at night, whiskey on his breath, and we could always hear the grunts and animal noises he made as he took from my mother the only self respect she had left on her old bed with the thread bare sheets. The guy was always hungry after they did what they did, and would make my mom warm up what little food we had left in the refrigerator, gorging his fat ass with no regard for any of us or what little we had. He was a two bit hustler, and an unlucky gambler, a general piece of shit as a human being. One night when I was just past 16 he came over for his weekly romp. It was right before Christmas and my mom had been saving for months so she could get us kids one small gift each, normally a nice under shirt or some brand new socks, and buy a small ham for our holiday meal. Bills had always taken what little money she had, but she worked extra jobs in the months before the holidays so at least we would always have a Christmas. She must have told Frank about her meager savings and one night when he was taking a crap just before he left, I heard her crying softly in the kitchen. I walked in and asked her what was wrong, and at first she wouldn't say. I said come on mom what's wrong, having no idea. She said that Frank had some debts from betting, and he had taken the money she had been putting away to pay them off. I must have looked angry and my mom pleaded with me to leave it alone. Frank was supposedly a tough guy and she was worried for my safety. I knew in that moment from the very depths of my soul that she was worrying for the wrong guy. I assured her that I would leave it alone. I kissed her on the forehead, grabbed my coat and told her I was going over to Jimmy's for a little while. When Frank came down the steps of our apartment he headed south to visit one of the local back alley gambling parlors, whistling along the way, and casually fondling the money he had taken from my mother in his right pants pocket. I followed him in the quiet darkness.

The night was getting cold and a slight rain was beginning to fall, and still I was patient. I was always patient. After a few hours Frank came walking out. From the smile on his face it must have been a good night, and from the barely detectable stagger in his step he must have had a little extra to drink. He passed by me hidden in the shadows, and as he did I quickly came up behind him, rag in my left hand, and a box cutter in my right. I stepped to him with a proficiency bred not from experience, but more from hatred and a little book knowledge on hand-to-hand combat. As I forced the dirty cloth over his mouth to block any sound, I quickly cut his throat from one side to the other, and then pushed him away from me. He turned around and faced me, and I wanted him to. He looked at me in horror as the realization of the end of his days came calling, and as he grabbed at his throat trying to stop the warm flow of his filthy existence, he slowly fell to his knees. Not such a tough guy after all I thought. I walked up to him, looked him straight in the eyes, and just before they closed, spit directly into his face. He went down, never having a fucking clue what just happened. I quickly went through his pockets, and to my surprise old Frankie had finally had a lucky night. There was a roll of cash in his pocket with almost three grand, which in the 60s was a lot of cash. He had a nice watch, and I couldn't believe this, a fucking gold and diamond wedding ring. I retrieved from him his no longer required wealth, whipped out my dick, and in a last piece of calm vengeance, pissed on his still warm body. Frank really was a piece of garbage, but my family was going to have a very nice Christmas.

Cutting into my steak I was beginning to bounce between my physical hunger and my increasing intrigue. The nice part was that both were sitting right in front of me. I slid a thin slice of the dry aged beef into my mouth, chewing very slowly to fully appreciate the simple, yet perfect production of it all. Tillman's aged all of their own beef, and this alone set them apart from every other steak joint anywhere close to Grand Rapids. They grilled every piece of the locally raised Black Angus with the respect and attention of a catholic priest giving someone their last rites, finishing it on the piping hot metal serving plate with a flash of brandy and a dollop of garlic butter. I've had a lot of sex in my day, a lot of really good sex, and honestly this steak was better than most of it. As I grabbed a forkful of their homemade French fries I looked across the table at Sam and said that perhaps we had a few things in common. I wasn't ready to drop my panties just yet, but I was beginning to believe that he was who he said he was. In this business you don't have much of a social life, and there are very few friends, so maybe it was the scotch, or maybe I had thoughts that deep down inside I'd been wanting to confide in someone, I don't know, but I began to tell him about my first. I didn't need to tell him any names, names can get you caught, or where it took place, just the general idea of what took place. He had no idea that I was raised in a Sicilian orphanage, and I was never going to reveal it in spite of my increasing comfort level. I just told him how a guy had tried to have his way with my first girl friend. We were both 12, and he was much older. That in itself was enough for me, but seeing the tears running down her innocent and now swollen face, and the torn dress that she always looked so pretty in had sealed the deal. I told him how I watched the man for a brief period, figured out where he was weak, and took care of it, plain and simple.

He asked me if I remembered how it felt and I said honestly I never really gave a damn. Life was very simple for me for as long as I could remember. If you were hungry you found food, if you were tired you slept, if you ran into a problem you fixed it, no bells and no whistles. He sat back and looked at me like he wasn't quite convinced. Again he smiled and asked what about the second one, did I feel anything, or was it just simple motor function like the first. As I thought back a slight smile came across my face, and I replied that the second, while similar in motivation, actually had felt slightly good. Good, he asked? Yes, good I said. The guy was a low life, piece of shit, dirt bag mother fucker, and he almost killed my brother. Being the one who caused his last breath in all honesty had felt good, actually great. For me it was the same way he said. That guy was fucking my mom, and fucking my whole family at the same time and I ended his ass. I did, a 16 year old kid with no training or back up, just brains and balls, and I took his life. We both sat there for a moment in complete silence. Call it a realization, male bonding, or something else, but we had just accepted who we were, maybe for the first time ever.

He said you know there are quite a few people in this business who actually get off on it. I agreed, took another drink, and nodded my head. For me though it was never like that. The jobs I did needed to be done. The thought of actually enjoying it always seemed like a big mistake. You needed to keep work and play separate, call it discipline, but for me it was also common sense. The people who liked this type of work were sociopaths and freaks, neither a label I would ever carry. In the beginning it was simply an evolution of anger, but as I got older and matured it became business, plain and simple. I won't say that I didn't have a signature to my work, and I could get creative if the job called for it, but meat and potato's were more my style, or whack'em and stack'em as some guys called it. Sam was more involved with the mental side of it I thought and asked me if I had had ever felt "drunk on power" so to speak from being able to take somebody out. I won't lie, it was at times a rush, but I always kept my emotions in check and that was my answer. Maybe it was age, and maybe it was experience, but he knew something that I had yet to be able to admit to myself. He challenged me on my answer and I thought who the fuck is this guy? He's been sitting here for all of an hour and he thinks he has me all figured out. I was started to get a little pissed, and sensing this he said look I'm not trying to play shrink, but there are many layers to anybody who does what we do, and as I've aged I've tried to make peace with as many of mine as I could. I'm just trying to suggest the same to you. You know when you first get involved with this it's as foreign as Chinese food, but what we don't know, or won't admit, is the attraction and the thirst it can create. Nodding my head he went on, it's like taking a drink of the devils wine. At first it may be just curiosity, and the taste is not what we expect, and yet we want another drink, even when we don't know it. That old bottle is sitting on the table and once we pop the cork there is no putting it back in, and the funny part is that we know in spite of the danger it contains, we are among the select few who can drink from it at will. Nobody and nothing tells us what we're going to do, how we will live, or when we will die. It is intoxicating, to say the least.

We both raised our glasses, toasting the undeniable truth of his words. As we sat the glass tumblers now empty of their contents back onto the table I placed a handful of bills down to pay the check, thanked Sam for the conversation and the wisdom, wished him well in the years to come, and walked out into the cool dark night.

One

Disgraziata! I will never forget this word as long as I live. How could anyone refer to children who had been dumped off in the orphanage as babies, left with no family, no future, and no past that we would ever be a part of, as a disgrace? We didn't choose to be born, and we sure didn't choose to be born illegitimately, but here we were just the same. We had the deck stacked against us right out of the gate, and those of us with any level of intelligence knew it. As a child I had the typical thoughts of most of the other orphans; why, was probably the big one for everyone. Had my parents just not wanted us? Was their some kind of mistake and our parents didn't know about us (we weren't familiar with biology yet)? Many of us had been sent here because of poverty or illegitimacy, and that was a hard pill to swallow. Thinking that your parents simply could not afford another child and opted to give you up, or thinking that you were simply bastard offspring was another one that no one wanted to consider. It was much easier to fantasize about the other possibilities, and that fantasy was a sugar coated escape from what we would come to deal with every day. In La Cass

Del Benefenicia life was what it was, and nothing more, unless you were willing to go out and get it.

Reality came in fast and hard if you lived in an orphanage. There was little room, time, or money for the typical soft existence that most children enjoy in their early life, but in a way my brother and I considered it a blessing. It taught us right from the start that life was not fair, not normally kind, and that if you wanted anything out of this world you were going to have to work your ass off to get it. That suited us just fine. We learned quick that we didn't like owing anybody, anything. Debt was a weakness that could be exploited and with the hand we had already been dealt in life we would suffer our fair share of exploitation already, we figured we sure as hell didn't need any help. We also learned that God had blessed us with an innate talent for survival. We were street smart and intelligent, and we quickly grew stronger both mentally and physically than the other kids around us, but we'll talk more about that later.

The nun who was in charge of accepting the babies when they first came to the orphanage was a middle aged woman named Sister Marie Chirco. I obviously don't remember her as a baby, but as we grew older I always noticed how she stood out in our world of hardship and uncertainty. She was kind to all of the children, and even when she would sternly reprimand us, or even occasionally crack us on the hand with the willow switch she always seemed to have, you still knew she cared about us, every one. Sister Marie was also in charge of giving us the name we would carry. I don't know how you get picked to do this, but I'm glad she had a talent for it. I hate to think what our names might have ended up being if we had been named by someone else. I was given the name Dominic Fortunata and my twin brother was named Diamo. Our last name in Italian meant "lucky", and this would eventually lead me to my first understanding of the word irony. When I got older I approached Sister Marie one day and inquired as to her choice of names considering our circumstances. She said two things, and to this day I believe she meant every word; first she said; if you are alive you are fortunate. Life is a gift, everything else is a privilege and don't you ever forget it. Second, she said that because even as babies she considered us as special, lucky was what the world would be with us in it. I never knew my mother, but in that instant and with those words, I knew for a moment how a child feels about their mother, it was my first feeling of love.

Our mother, from what we were told later, was a beautiful Sicilian woman, with raven black hair, fire in her eyes, and a heart that reached out to everyone. She was a princess without the official title. The middle daughter of a prominent and wealthy family, who they said walked through the streets of Floridia with her head held high, a confident, radiant and blazon beauty, with a spirit that seemed to scent the air around her like the pungent lemon tress and lavender that grew thick on the Sicilian hillsides.

The children would swarm at her feet as she walked through the city square, smitten by her beauty, or perhaps just caught up in the radiant energy that she put out to the world around her. She was wise and kind beyond her age and would often sit and talk with the less fortunate street people, many times offering to share her lunch or the little money she carried with her. As kind as she was she also carried the blood of her people and like them, was no one to be trifled with or disrespected. It was said that one time one of the older men who had apparently taken too much to drink, to early in the day, decided to test his favor with her. In the end He hobbled away with less of his pride, less of his blood, and a scar on his left cheek that would tell the story for him for years to come. People would say that for all of the love and kindness she possessed, "Darla Chia De Armante" was a force to be reckoned with, even at a young age. Unfortunately this "women" was also in reality only a girl of 16, unfamiliar with the often lecherous tactics of tainted romance, and was soon to become pregnant by a traveling business man from a small manufacturing province in Russia, who would promise to marry her in order to get into her virgin panties, but would soon disappear like the swallows of Capistrano on the approaching fall winds.

The whole situation presented a serious problem for our mother and her family. Being pregnant out of wedlock was bad enough, but having been impregnated by not only a Russian, but one who had left the country, made the inevitable decision of giving us up pretty much etched in stone. I don't think my mother ever wanted to do it, no true Sicilian women would, but she was young and Grandfather was the head of the family. So it was done.

Two

There are a lot of misconceptions out there about being a *hit man*. Most of what people believe is just glorified Hollywood fluff simply intended to help sell movies. In truth for most of the people I've worked with in any capacity, it's just a job. The world has lots of problems and the people who solve those problems have particular job skills to do so. If you have a leaking faucet you call a plumber. If you need to buy some steaks, you go to a butcher. If you need a *removal*, you contact somebody like me.

I have always referred to the work I do as a removal. Why, you may ask? It sounds so cold and impersonal, and guess what, that's because for a true professional, it is. It's been going on since the existence of mankind and believe me nothing is going to change anytime soon. The world has lots of people in it, and not all of us are contributing citizens. You have *good* people and *bad* people and unfortunately the numbers tend to tip in a southern direction with something as basic and constant as the economic climate. I used to try and think that everyone of us was basically good, and that people sometimes had rough lives and it caused them to change as people and do the bad things that they would come to do. That's complete bullshit. People are either born with *malicia* in their eyes or they are not. It's that simple. You can have a child born with a pre-planned life of hard knocks ahead of them, the worst of the worst, and yet as they grow if that child was born with good inside, that good will stay alive in spite of all the crap they will come to endure. It may be protected by a rough exterior, bad habits, or tough talk, but for the strongest it will remain as protected as a new born.

On the flip side if you have an individual born under a bad sign, there is rarely anything you can do to change it. Basically a shithead, is a shithead, is a shithead. They can be born with the best of circumstances, with loving parents and nurturing surroundings. They can be encouraged by the people in their life while growing up. They can be immersed in love, carrying, and spiritual nourishment, and be given the gifts of King Solomon. They can have it all, and still the darkness will remain. This fact of life, while being negative in its essence has a positive side to it; it assures a certain level of job security for those in my profession.

I did my first removal at the age of 12, and it was for love, not money. There's a big difference. One thing I can tell you, if you have a "button" placed on you, you are much better off if it's just business and not personal. If it's business it might be negotiable or rectifiable. It could have been a misunderstanding, and misunderstandings can be corrected. At some level it is possible to be de-escalated or even called off, but not if its personal. Angelia

Triano was my first love, a beautiful and untarnished Sicilian girl of only 12, and an innocent. She was a flower in a field of sewage, a gift to those who called her friend, and bottom line she was just a kid. Senor Fredo Di Piazza was a drunk and a lecher who not only took advantage of her age and her innocence, he poisoned her very soul by the depravity he would choose to impose on her, and for that he would lose his life.

Angelia was left at La Cassa Della Beneficenza orphanage as a baby, and like the rest of us this world was to be the only life she would know as a child. Living in an orphanage goes in various stages of acceptance and comprehending. As a baby you obviously don't understand anything around you. You eat, sleep, poop, cry, and are occasionally held, but overall you are protected and life is warm and safe. As you become a child you start to learn about your own responsibility to look out for yourself, those that don't become easy targets. The years in an orphanage bounce intermittently between the wonder and amazement of childhood, and the stark reality of what man is capable of. For most children in the world you have a mother and father, some family and possibly a few siblings. By genetics or just by design you have a certain level of protection that you come to expect. Not if you're in an orphanage. The people that look out for you, or are supposed to, are paid to do so. To a large extent they have no moral obligation to choose between right and wrong about anything, it's just their job and they go by the rules with little or nothing else freely given. There are exceptions to this rule, and thank God for that, but not many. A simple fact of life is that the staff in an orphanage, and most of the people you will meet, go through daily life with their own best interests in mind, and not yours. In spite of this, Angelia remained pure. She wasn't bitter or cynical. She was warm and kind. She shared her meager possessions with the other kids who had so little. She looked out for the younger children and helped the nuns with the babies. Many times when a child of the orphanage had found themselves crying and sad, she would console them, hug them, and make them feel like someone actually cared. She was a beautiful and wonderful girl and in many instances the closest thing to family that some of these kids would ever have, and Senor Di Piazza had come to notice her.

What he didn't realize was that I had noticed him too.

Senor Di Piazza was in charge of maintenance at the orphanage and lived on the grounds. This enabled him to handle problems that might occur within the facility in a timely fashion, and without the inconvenience and wasted efforts of having to be called in from farther away. He lived alone in a small stone house that had been built in the back hillside of the large orphanage many years ago. The home was small and modestly built, but had a beautiful garden planted with tomatoes, eggplant, grapes and strawberries, lemon and olive trees, several different types of basil and herbs, and many other varieties of plants and trees that would all flourish in the warm Sicilian summer. He had a fireplace made out of field stone with a built in cast iron cooking pot on a swing arm. Many times in the winter we could smell the aroma of a Sicilian stew that he was fond of making. One time I had asked him what was in it that smelled so wonderful–and which he would never offer to any of us. He told me that it was an old recipe of his grandmother's comprised of lamb, chicken, pancetta, garlic, leeks, potatoes, basil, tomatoes, lemon juice and first pressed virgin olive oil from his own orchard. He would drift off in his eyes as he described the process to me; first you sautéed the chopped up lamb, chicken, and pancetta in the fresh pressed olive oil. Over the fire it would sizzle and pop as the fat from the oils caramelized the meat. When it was browned you would add the garlic and leeks and cook them down to a butter-like texture that added their rich, sweet, and pungent flavor to the mix. Next you would add the diced potatoes, letting them brown in the juices of the sizzling kettle. Finally he added the ripe tomatoes that exploded with juice as you cut them, aromatic basil, that would leave a slight lingering scent of licorice on your fingers as you held it, and the tart sweet fresh lemon juice which you could actually taste the sunshine in. He described how he would top it off with a small bit of sea salt, and occasionally a handful of chopped fennel he had just picked from the garden, cover it up and let it simmer down for hours to come, off to the side of the fire in the low heat. He described how he always started the meal with an antipasto of prosciutto or sopressata, fresh mozzarella and a local farmers cheese, mixed olives and peppers, and a loaf of fresh baked semolina bread, all of it washed down with plenty of the dark red wine from the nearby vineyards. Compared to the gruel we were expected to survive on this was pure heaven. I hated him for not sharing, and I hated him even more for describing the feast in such vivid detail, but at the same time I loved to hear the story and would come to ask him to repeat it on many occasions. It temporarily took me out of my existence, if only for a little while, and that was a luxury that I needed even if it meant I had to endure someone like Senor Piazza.

The food that we lived on was basic and seasonal. We had a lot of orzo, pasta, bread and porridge. They were all very cheap, in large supply, and could be made to go a long way. They would cook the orzo and pasta with different vegetable tossed in, and normally tomatoes and garlic, or cream and whatever cheese was available, with a little bit of salt and not much else. We ate very little meat because it was expensive and we had no refrigeration, but we always had an abundant supply of fresh baked bread. It was delicious, even a couple days old, and we would often dip the slices in olive oil, or spread it with a spoonful of the local lavender honey. Occasionally, we would be given a treat of bread, cream, and sugar, which was occasionally topped with a spoonful of mascarpone. For us it was like having dessert for supper. I first thought that it was because the nuns had wanted to do something nice for us orphans, but I soon figured out that the only reason they did it was when they ran out of the normal food, or were simply too lazy to cook.

In the colder times they would occasionally make us dishes with sundried tomatoes and cured calamata olives which had been packed in oil and salt to keep over the winter. The tomatoes were loaded with vitamin C which they said kept you from getting sick, and the olives were packed with nutrients from the oil that they rested in; but the main reason we had them was because they were cheap. Somebody told me once that in America these were considered gourmet food that people would pay big money for. It struck me as very funny because to us it was considered peasant food that most Sicilians wouldn't even think of eating. The nuns that were in charge of the kitchen basically looked at cooking as a duty and nothing more. They made the same stuff over and over with little variation to speak of; it was just another task. This also struck me as very funny and I assumed that not one of them could have been born in Sicily because for me it was simply not possible that any true Sicilian women could have ever cooked with such a lack of passion. Even as a young boy I thought to myself that they must have possessed the same skills in bed, or lack thereof, and that's why they had become nuns.

In the summer we did enjoy some of the produce that we grew on the grounds, but the best of it was sold to the local markets to make money for the orphanage. We basically lived in a no frills existence and were always told to be grateful for it.

Sometimes when we had our meals I would dream of the conversations about food I had had with Senor Piazza. I would envision me, my brother Diamo, and Angelia all living together in the stone house with the wonderful garden and the warm stone fireplace. I envisioned us laughing and cooking and harvesting the fruits and vegetables that we would enjoy. It was absolute bliss, if only for that moment. Senor Di piazza's house also had a veranda off the kitchen that overlooked the Floridian countryside. The house was built on the side of a hill and the veranda had also been built out of stone with a slate patio, and a short stone wall that extended along the entire back end. The wall I assumed was intended to keep anyone who was out on the veranda from accidently stepping over, as it was a pretty long distance to the rocky ground below.

I had noticed this as well.

Three

Most of our time at the orphanage was spent either in school, doing chores, or attending church, but as we grew older we learned that if you got your work and school work done quickly you could have more free time. Diamo and I soon figured out that if we were ever going to have a better life, either while in the orphanage, or after it, we would need to make money. At first we would sneak out, sometimes at night, and steal fruit from the orchards in the surrounding hills. We would go to one place and gather lemons and Sicilian red oranges, visiting another for sweet montagnola and tardiva peaches and crisp apples, and yet another for plums, melons, and the tiny sweet strawberry that marked the beginning of summer. We would come back with the old burlap sacks stuffed with goods, and as fruit was not something we got a lot of it made us quite popular in a short time. One of the older boys came to me soon after we started and told me that he would tell the nuns if we did not give him extra fruit. After pondering his request I agreed, telling him that it would have to be done in private so that the other kids would not start the same thing or get jealous. I told him to meet me the next day after supper in the woods behind the storage building in the back of the orphanage, and told him to bring a large sack and a long piece of rope to secure his new found bounty. The best place to hide it, and hide it you must, was in the woods or somewhere on the grounds. You couldn't just leave it under your bed or someplace similar for fear of being discovered by the nuns, or having it stolen by the other kids. After our evening meal he showed up as expected. When he saw that I had brought no fruit or anything else he quickly got angry and said he was going directly to the nuns. As he turned to run, Diamo, who was now standing behind him, punched him right in the stomach. As he doubled over in pain and now out of breath, we both pummeled him with our fists, feet, and an old ax handle that I had stolen from the garden shed. I secured his hands and feet with two pieces of rope, tied an old piece of cloth around his mouth so he could not talk, and as I crouched down to look him in his trembling face, said listen to me very carefully...

You're not getting any of our fruit or anything else. You are going to spend the night out here to think about what you want to do when we come back, or should I say if we come back. It's not supposed to rain this evening, but it will be cold. As you spend the night out here all by yourself you had better think about what your greed has cost you, and who you're dealing with. In the morning I may give you one chance to convince me that we can trust you to keep your mouth shut. If not we will hang you from that big oak tree over there, with the very rope that you brought.

I am also going to pour a mixture of fresh cows blood (saying it was fresh was Diamo's idea) and honey in the woods around you. What this will do is bring in the wild animals during the night to keep you company. If we do not come to an agreement, before we hang you we will leave you here for another night, and this time the blood and honey will be on you, and not the ground. Know this, not you or anybody else will ever steal from me and my brother without paying the price. Nod if you understand, to which he did. I placed the sack he had brought along over his head and shoulders, walked in a wide circle around him, pouring out the jug of water we had brought along so that he could hear it hit the earth, and walked off to the shelter of our building. The next morning after our usual bad breakfast we went back to the woods to find our friend right where we had left him, damp and shivering. Not only did he agree to our terms, in time he became one of our workers and we never had another problem from him.

We were only nine when we started hustling, and nervous as hell of being caught, but the fear of this was soon overshadowed by the joy of our increasing wealth, and as we got older we began to branch out. As I said before we were both physically stronger than the other kids, and one day I observed how the men who carried the products from our orphanage to sell on the streets of Floridia, would always strain under the heavy bags and crates, loading fruits and vegetables into a wagon in the hot summer sun. After watching them for some time, one day we offered to help them load the trailer. The head Capo said that we were too young, and too weak, and would not be able to lift the heavy goods off the ground, much less into the trailer. I bowed my head, grinning at Diamo, and looked back up and said please sir, my brother and I are good workers and we just want to help. He looked at me and said you can't even get one of these bags of potatoes into the trailer, now stop bothering us. I'll wager you ten Lira that I can lift ten bags of potatoes into that trailer! He looked at me and said boy what did you just say? I repeated myself and he quickly came to stand over me as he angrily scorned me both for my arrogance, and for the very suggestion of gambling. I should turn you into the head nun for your wicked ways! Does this mean you will not accept my bet, I said? What he didn't realize was that kids see and hear everything. I had overheard him many times talking about the pretty girls at the market, his wife's bad cooking, and the many different games he liked to bet on (and was not very good.) I knew he would take the bet. I just had to stand my ground, and quicker than I imagined he said he boasted that he would indeed accept my wager, and my money soon after words.

Just for show I grabbed the first bag and pretended to have difficulty lifting it off the ground, to which he and the other men chided me, asking if I was ready to quit and go back to our child's play. As they laughed at me and slapped each other on the back Diamo said I know he can do it, and I'll double the wager to prove it. This was way too easy, and the man quickly agreed.

One of the other workers wanted to bet as well, but we thought better of it than to accept. It was a con job, plain and simple, but pissing off one guy was a lot easier than having to deal with two. I was going to actually throw the bags into the cart to embarrass the man, but as I looked at Diamo we both realized this would be foolish on our point, so slowly, and methodically, with as much faked strain as I could muster, I loaded all ten bags into the now half full wagon. I did a good job of acting and the man just stood there in disbelief at the revelation that not only had I done it, but also that we were now owed 20 of his hard earned Lira. At first he said he would not pay, and that we had tricked him, but one of the other men stepped in and said that if he did not honor his bets, especially with an orphan, no one would ever allow him to wager again. In Sicily there are rules to everything in life. Some are written, and some are not, and one of the oldest unwritten rules is that you pay your bets, win or lose. For all of its beauty and magnificence this country was also as cold as the winter snow when it came to matters of money, and anyone who didn't respect this fact was soon made quite aware of it with either their money or there life.

His 20 was really the furthest thing from our minds from the very beginning, but I had to play it smart. Mister, I said, forget the 20, we just want work. He looked at me for a moment and said that we were much too young, to which Diamo replied that we had proven him wrong on that already. Why do you want to do this hard work he asked? The real reason was to be able to expand our operations to the nearby docks and city, but I just said we wanted to make a little money. We earn nothing at the orphanage and it takes money to buy candy for the pretty girls. He looked at us for a moment, looked at his co-workers, and busted out into a huge belly laugh as he said girls, it always comes down to getting the girls yes? It was a smart move. He would save face, and the 20 Lira if he agreed, and his work would now become much easier. He would pay us a pittance, and we knew it, but that's not where the real money was, and we knew this as well. The other men also started laughing and came over and slapped us both on the back. In that moment we became employed, and accepted, both of which would prove to be very valuable in the future. We quickly showed ourselves to be both eager and able at our new job, and Arturo the boss greatly appreciated the help. We started spending more and more time bringing the goods to market and to the local shops, all the while watching everything around us.

Floridia was located in the Sardinia province of Sicily and had a large waterfront nearby where the American navy would dock their ships to refuel, resupply, and allow the GI's to go on shore leave. As kids we were able to approach anyone without alarm and we soon struck up conversations with the sailors about America, sailing, and what their life was like on the ship. They would give us American chocolate bars, which was kind of funny to us as Italian chocolate was much better, but we accepted it graciously.

What we found with the chocolate and soon other things was that local people would buy it just because it came from America. We began to ask the sailors about cigarettes and blue jeans. They each had a ration card and were allowed to purchase liquor, cigarettes, and other things in quantities only available to them and at a very inexpensive cost. We asked them one day about buying there extra cigarettes and the first guy gave us a little shit over smoking at our age. When he saw we had money and were quite serious he no longer gave us any shit. We started buying from any of the sailors that would sell, and we soon amassed a small fortune in black-market goods which we always doubled, or tripled our money on. Italian men loved American whiskey and smokes and could not seem to get enough of Jack Daniels and Marlboros, even at a hefty price. We dabbled a little in jeans and small appliances like toasters and American coffee makers, but the electric systems in Sicily versus America made it kind of a pain, so we soon quit and focused only on liquor and tobacco. We had quite an operation going and we were smart and gave our boss a weekly pay off from our stash of contraband. He didn't know much, and he didn't need to. He got his stuff every week like clockwork and everyone was happy.

One evening after returning from another successful trip to the docks I noticed Angelina sitting under a tree, crying and looking quite upset. She was not only my girlfriend but my shelter from the rough life that we lived in and I felt the need to protect her from the world just as a shepherd would protect his sheep from the wolves. She had been crying and her face looked as if she had been hit. Her beautiful white dress was torn at the collar and her knees were scraped. I could feel my face begin to turn warm as I asked her to tell me what had happened. In a soft and slightly broken tone she explained to me how she had been helping Senor Di Piazza during the afternoon and he had invited her to join him for a cool beverage after all of their hard work. They had gone back to his villa and he had poured them both a glass of the homemade red wine that he was so fond of. She had asked if she could have perhaps lemonade or milk as she did not enjoy the strong taste of alcohol, to which he had replied that if she was ever going to be a women, and not a little girl, she would need to learn to enjoy some new things. She said that she was confused as to what he had meant, but when he came and sat next to her, placing his dirty hand on her inner thigh, she knew in an instant what he had in mind. She asked him to stop but he continued, touching her all over her young body and becoming quite excited. She stood to leave and he forcefully told her to sit down and grabbed her arm. Now she was really scared and started to run, but he caught her by the collar of her dress and threw her to the cobblestone floor as he laughed and said he would make her a women. Fortunately, she was faster than him and with the combination of his age and excessive weight she was able to escape what he had in mind. As she ran out the door he called her a Butonna, or whore in Italian and told her to come back when she was a women!

She asked what we should do and she was very afraid. She wanted to tell the nuns, but I explained that they would not believe her and it would probably make things worse for her anyway. What do I do then Dominick? I am afraid now and if he tries again maybe this time I am not so fast and he hurts me. I told her not to worry, not to be alone with him ever again, to tell no one else, and that I would take care of it. She looked at me with an expression of slight disbelief, and I again assured her that I would take care of it. I pulled her close to me and wrapped my arms around her and I could feel her start to calm down as we talked about the ships and the market. I told her that I would buy her a new dress the very next day and to throw away the one that she had been wearing so she would never have to look at it again. After dropping her off at her building I spent the rest of the night smoking, thinking, and making my plans for Señor Di Piazza.

———————————————

Four

I waited a week to let the whole situation settle down and then came up with what I thought was a pretty good plan. Every night after supper I would climb into the woods that overlooked his house and watch. I had picked a spot where I would be hidden from sight, but could easily see into the windows of the stone house with only a slight adjustment of my position and could also observe the garden and the veranda off the back end. I noticed things that he did every evening. He would get home, hang his jacket from a hook on the front porch, and go to the kitchen to wash his hands before anything else. He would then vary between working a little in the garden, reading, or listening to music, and he always started with a glass of wine. He would eventually begin to cook his late meal, or sometimes would simply make a tray of bread and meat with some pickles or olives on the side. Every night just before bed he would take out a cloth bag from someplace behind the kitchen cupboard and would then sit at the small table spending a great deal of time with whatever it was. I was too far away to see it clearly but assumed it must be important as he doted over it much like a father with a young child.

He would then put it back into its hiding place, look around as if someone were watching, and retire for the night.

One afternoon I approached him as he was heading home. I engaged him with small talk as we walked, telling him how much I had learned from him about both working and cooking in the past. I was trying to stroke his ego to make my job easier but I had caught him on a day where he was in a bad mood and he spoke gruffly and dismissed my compliment with indifference and a scowl. I let it go and left him alone, knowing his arrogance would eventually bite on the compliments I had given. I was right and two days later he approached me with a smile and much better disposition. He was quite jovial, apparently not hung over as usual, and spoke gleefully about the weather and the upcoming festivals of wine. He complimented me and said that he respected the fact that both me and my brother were not only tough, but unafraid to get our hands dirty. He had no idea how right he was.

Later in the week I asked him if I could help pick vegetables in his garden and he agreed and told me to come by the next afternoon. I knew he liked to drink, and I assumed he enjoyed whiskey like the other men, so I brought along a bottle of Johnnie Walker Black from our stash. He was both excited and surprised and asked me how a boy my age had gotten something so valuable and hard to obtain. I told him about working with Arturo in the city and I made up a lie telling him how an American sailor had given it to me knowing that I lived in an orphanage and directing me to trade it for food or something else I needed. I told him it was my gift to him, but that a little fruit from his orchard and maybe some cheese would most certainly be appreciated. He got a look of both joy and greed in his eyes as he said sure, we can work something out. He planned on ripping me off from the very start, assuming that as a kid I had no idea what it was worth on the streets. I was aware of what his response would be well before I ever showed him the bottle. What he had let his arrogance blind him to was that I knew exactly its value, but also that it was much also stronger than the Sicilian wine he was used to and would make him drunk very quickly, and a soft target for what I had in mind. In Sicily we have a saying that every gift has a price, Señor Di Piazza had allowed his greed to let him forget this.

We walked into the garden and he showed me tomatoes, figs, and lemons that were ready for harvesting. He gave me a medium sized basket to put them in and excused himself to get glasses for the scotch. I began to pick some fruit and heard him come back a short time later with the glasses and a tray of bread and cheese. He poured himself a healthy amount of the free whiskey, offering me a small splash as well, and sat down to watch me work. After I had filled my basket I went and sat with him, breaking off a piece of the bread and sipping the liquor. He had brought out a carafe of water which I poured generously into my glass to dilute the scotch. He laughed and said you haven't acquired a taste for it yet Dominick, but like other things you will? We talked for a while longer and then I asked if we could watch the sunset off his back veranda as I knew he did every night. He agreed and as we moved our things to the back of the house I deliberately placed our chairs close to the stone wall overlooking the valley below. Señor Di Piazza warned me to be careful as falling over the steep drop might certainly end my young life. I agreed, thanking him for his concern, and assured him that I would be very careful, but that is was so beautiful I just wanted to see it as closely as possible. He laughed and said be careful of getting to close to things of beauty my friend, for they can be the most dangerous. Again I agreed and asked him if I could refill his now empty glass. As we sat for a while longer he told me stories of his childhood and about the many women he had known. He failed to mention his taste in young girls, but this would be dealt with soon enough.

I continued to refill the glass with no objections from him, and as the whiskey took its effect and the sun began to sink, I excused myself to use the bathroom. As I walked back to join him he had his back to me and was completely consumed by the view and the drink, just as I had expected. I had picked up a small brown brick from the ground and easily walked up behind him, striking him directly in the back of his skull as he looked off into the distance. To my surprise he made no sound, just leaning over with his head tilted to the side. With his thick hair I could not see any blood but I wanted to be sure and I hit him again in the same spot. As I walked around in front of him he appeared as if he had fallen asleep with his head now resting on his chest, still rising intermittently with shallow breaths. I stepped to the wall behind me sizing up the distance I would have to drag his now limp body and thinking in my head how to get him over it without joining him in the process. I considered the easiest way was probably to just grab him around the waist from the front, letting his arms and head drape over me while I lifted and pulled him the few feet. He weighed a lot, but my fear and anger had given me strength I had never known before and I found the task much easier than expected. I had to turn to sit him on the ledge and again paused to make sure I had my plan correct. Holding him up while he sat on the edge of the wall was now easy and as I pondered my reasons for doing what I was about to do, I lost any reservations I may have had. With both hands I gave him a hard shove and gravity did the rest as he tumbled through the air for just a few seconds and then landed on the rocks below with his head and shoulders taking the force of the fall. As he lay in a crumpled pile at the bottom I could now see crimson liquid starting to seep out into the rocks around him and I knew he was dead.

I paused for a second and sat down with my glass of water to collect my thoughts. No one usually visited the home so I wasn't in a hurry at all and I wanted to think the whole thing through again before I left. Suddenly, I remembered the bag behind the kitchen cupboard and as my curiosity got the better of me I decided to go get it. It took a few minutes of moving glasses and jars to find the small secret panel that had obviously been designed to protect its hidden contents, but it had just a tiny handle with no lock and I easily opened it. Inside was the well worn canvass bag and as I pulled it out I could feel the weight of the contents, now heavy in my hand. I untied the piece of rope that was keeping the bag closed and dumped the shiny coins out onto the kitchen table. By now there wasn't much light, but even in the darkness I could see that they were gold and all of the size of a small thin cookie. I quickly counted 27 pieces in all and was starting to get really excited at the fortune I had just found, but I brought myself back to the moment, returning them to the bag, and tying it securely. I went back to the veranda and thought again for a moment. I wanted it to look like Señor Di Piazza had simply fallen over the wall in his well known and common state of intoxication so first I tossed his glass over to shatter on the stones around him. Next I made the veranda appear as if he had been alone, returning my glass to the kitchen, washing and drying it and placing it back in the cupboard. I looked on the floor of the patio for any blood which I already knew was not there. I wanted to bring the fruit and vegetables back with me but I knew that this would have to be explained, and besides with the gold I had found I could afford both in quantity for quite some time. I locked the front door from the inside, climbed out a side window, and made my way back to our building quietly in the darkness without ever being seen.

The next afternoon when Señor Di Piazza had not shown up to do his work as usual the nuns sent someone to his house. When he did not answer the head nun and the monsignor decided to go there in person and having a key were able to let themselves in. After a brief search of the place they discovered his body lying on the rocks below and quickly got some of the other workers to retrieve him. After seeing the broken glass, the bottle of scotch, now almost empty on the veranda table, they put two and two together and simply notified his next of kin. It was the 1970's and rural Sicily where death was as common as life and DNA technology did not exist. This combined with his afore mentioned lifestyle, insured that there would be no investigation, just a simple funeral. Probably the biggest issue was that the orphanage had to now find a new caretaker. Nothing else was ever said about it and no questions remained.

———————————

Five

In 1978 the Italian premier was kidnapped in Rome by a secondary faction of the red brigade. During the process his five body guards and a few innocent bystanders were killed from the gunfire and grenades that were used in the attack. Sean O'Shannon and his wife Lilly had recently arrived from Ireland and were two of the people killed. Their young son Sean Jr. was wounded but would recover. He had suffered some temporary hearing loss and post traumatic shock, which when combined made him appear to be incoherent and incapable of speaking by those who would try to interview the young man in the days to follow. The truth of the matter was that Sean and his parents had recently fled from Limerick to Italy after his father had witnessed a brutal murder by one of the local crime families. Limerick was the third largest city in Ireland and being situated in the Midwest region was very popular for its scenery, music, and historic local architecture. The people were many generations deep with everything from cobblers and shepherds to students and factory workers. The Irish have always been a hard working lot, but unemployment had become rampant, and the babies had to be fed, so many of them who didn't really want to live the hard life had ended up there just the same. Unless you lived there you would never have known that loan sharking, heroin, extortion, and contract killings by the continually warring factions was just as common as anything else. Sean's father was fortunate and had been a local shopkeeper, and his mother a doting stay at home mum, until the Friday that his dad had closed up shop early and had gone to the milk market to buy some fresh produce. As is common in life, things can change in just the blink of an eye, and Sean Sr. chose to walk down the wrong alley on his way home, making him the one and only witness to a murder committed by none other than Michael Dalcassian.

The Dalcassian's controlled all activity on the north side of the river Shannon and were well known for both their vicious tactics and the cold blooded way in which they maintained their business interests. Michael was the next in line for the throne and anyone that could threaten that succession would never be allowed to survive. Sean Sr. was never going to talk. You just didn't if you had any common sense, but he knew that the crime family would never believe this, and his days were certainly numbered, as well those of his family. He had saved his entire life, and was able to quickly strike a deal with a competing business man who had wanted to buy his shop for many years now. In the middle of the night he, his wife, and their only son, had escaped Ireland in hopes of starting over in another place. They had unfortunately been in the wrong place, at the wrong time, and their young son would now be made to fend for himself in a country far from home.

While in the hospital he slowly began to remember what had happened and in spite of his great sadness over losing his mum and dad he knew to keep his mouth shut about where he was from. Italy wasn't that far from Ireland and he knew the Dalcassians were looking for his family, so he used the non speaking angle to his advantage. He had overheard the doctors talking with some government people, and surmised that they thought he was American not Irish, but they had no idea from what part. His father and mother had disposed of their Irish identification upon arrival and young Sean had none to begin with, so figuring out who he was or where he was from was completely in the control of the young man himself, and his lips were sealed. After his wounds had healed the local police were of the position that for the his safety as a potential witness he would need to be brought far away from Rome, and an orphanage was both the logical and practical answer, so he came to live with us.

I remember the day he showed up. He was shorter than the rest of the kids his age, and did not speak our language or any other, so some of the kids began picking on him and hitting him. They started to do it more and more until one day Sean fought back, and in spite of his engrained ferocity took a beating just the same. We weren't going to get involved. He wasn't our problem and he wasn't our friend, but I never liked bullies, and I particularly did not like the guys who picked on him, so one day when a few of them had decided to use him for sport once again Diamo and I decided to help him out. Sean was tough enough and knew how to fight, the numbers had just been against him up until now, yet he fought every time just the same. With his new found support the tide quickly changed and his attackers were now left in the dirt with bloodied noses and a clear lesson to never mess with him again. Once things settled and everyone had left he looked me in the eye, stuck out his right hand, and said thank you with a soft Irish accent. I looked at my brother with a surprised look on my face and Sean began to explain a little of his situation. It had been six months since he first came to us and I always thought what a relief it must have been for him to finally find a friend. We quickly realized that the three of us had much in common. We all liked hustling, relying on our wits instead of a hand out, and taking shit from no one. Ours would be a friendship that would grow in years to come and we would become each other's family. We got Sean hired on with us loading the trucks and he soon began showing us angles that we had never considered before. Limerick bears many similarities to Floridia, not so much in appearance, but in composition and social structure. Sean, although raised by good and honest parents, had street sense and a keen eye and could spot an opportunity as quickly, and sometimes quicker, than we could. We had been selling our booze to the locals, and at a good mark up. Sean noticed the tourist trade and the hotels and suggested that we try bringing our goods around to the managers of the kitchens and hotel bars, who would buy our liquor and cigarettes at a better price than we were currently getting, and would then sell it to the guests for an ever greater price and were happy to pay it. With our new found profits and a third partner we began our own little numbers racket, modeled much like the ones that the gangsters in America had. We kept a low profile on this part of our business as we did not want to attract the attention of the local carbineri, or Italian police. A little bit of whiskey and smoke peddling was one thing and we didn't do that much of it to get noticed. Gambling was another thing all together. If people won they bragged, if they lost they bitched, either way they talked, any when people talk too much, other people get caught. We had noticed other areas where we could probably have expanded into, but we were making enough and were smart enough not to let greed cloud our instincts, so we just kept doing what we were doing.

We had always given Arturo an occasional bit of our action from black marketing, but he soon figured out the numbers were bringing in more than the booze and he wanted a cut of this as well. It was a bit of a balancing act. We wanted to keep him happy, but we didn't want to get fucked in the process, and we told him as much. I told him that if we were going to have to do all the work and give a piece to everyone else around us we might as well shut it down and just stick with the cigarettes and whiskey. He protested a little, but he knew he had a good thing going and agreed that maybe we could throw him an extra fifth of scotch here and there and that would be enough. Just don't forget your old friend Arturo he'd say. We assured him we would not. Situation solved, and our numbers money was protected. We really wouldn't have had a problem giving him some of it, we made plenty, but we knew that once that door opened it would be hard to shut and before you know it the other bosses and who knew who else would be trying to shake us down. We ran our game a little different from the others in our town. For starters, we let people bet much smaller which didn't really matter in the end. A gambler is a gambler, and giving them a lower limit just allows them to bet more frequently. In the end their small coin bets turned into dollar size profits and they spend just as much, and sometimes even more because it doesn't seem to them like they are spending anything more than pocket change. We kept quiet and made it a point to avoid the bigger customers of the local Cosa Nostra families. We wouldn't even take their bets, and there were many opportunities to do it. We were just kids, but we were still taking money off the streets and needed to be careful not to piss the wrong people off and we always kept this in mind.

One day while I was sitting on a bench by the fish market, eating a bag of roasted nuts I had just purchased from a street vendor, a man came up and asked me if I was Dominick Fortunato.

I loved sitting here in the park and watching the many song birds fly about while crooning their calls of amore. It was my private time and I really did not want to share it, but I knew from my instincts and my eyes that this was not a man who would take disrespect kindly. I hesitated for a second and looked around to see if he had muscle backing him up. I wondered if he was a cop, but he didn't act, look, or dress like one and I nodded my head and said that I was. He asked if he could sit down and I cautiously agreed and slid over a little bit to give him room. Nice day he said, I nodded again and said yes it is. He asked if I knew who he was and I said that I did not. I had figured out by now that he was at minimum a boss, and possibly a captain or even a Don, from the looks of his clothes and shoes. He wore handmade Italian loafers that cost more than we made in three months, grey wool slacks and a silk shirt to match. He was confident, but not in an arrogant way, and I thought that he was obviously very comfortable with both the power he held, and the place where he held it. He said my name is Armando Bruno and I have been watching you and your friends for a while now, and I am impressed. He asked my age and I told him as he smiled to himself. He said that he wished all of his men were half as smart and hard working as us for he would be very wealthy if they were. I knew he was already very well off, but kept my mouth shut. He knew about the liquor and tobacco and had been hearing more and more about our small gambling enterprise, but he didn't ask for a tribute, or cut. He said that he respected both the fact that we were orphans and that we weren't afraid to hustle a buck, but said you can't get any bigger. Other families are starting to notice, and even though you're just kids you still have to know your place and be aware that you're taking money away from them, and nobody likes to lose money. I agreed quickly and he said good, I knew you were both a reasonable man and a smart one as he offered his hand to seal our agreement. As he got up to leave he gave me a white linen business card and asked that I come see him the following Monday for lunch. I told him that my brother and Sean were my partners and asked if I could bring them as well. He smiled and said no, just you for now and then maybe later I will meet your associates. He shook my hand once more, said I will look forward to seeing you next week, and walked away. Later that day I repeated my conversation to my brother and Sean and we all agreed that it might come in handy in the future and laughed about our continuing good fortune.

Sean began occasionally wondering about his family back in Ireland. He had uncles, aunts, cousins and friends, and in spite of our love for one another began missing his homeland more and more. He maintained his silence around other people, but when it was just the three of us we all shared the thoughts and dreams of young men, our hopes and our fears, and what we wanted to be someday. Sean wanted to go back to Limerick, get married, have a family, and buy his father's shop back. Diamo wanted to go to America, attend college, and become a doctor and help people. I didn't really know what I wanted to do. America sounded nice and I would not want to live anywhere without my brother. Maybe we could move there someday and Diamo could become a doctor and I would open a real Italian restaurant where we would cook the recipes from our homeland, drink rich red wine, and maybe hire a man to play piano during the evenings and serenade the guests with the wonderful Italian ballads and songs that we had grown up with.

I didn't know what the future would bring, but life was good. I had Diamo, Angelia, Sean, and now a new friend, so I chose not to spend my night worrying about it.

Six

The next Monday I visited Armando for lunch as I had agreed. His wife was preparing the meal, but like all Sicilian men he was also very skilled in the cugina. Women always cooked for a meeting of any size, while the men transacted business. It was in no way a disrespect thing, but the women were not typically involved in negotiations and it just made sense to leave them to be in charge of the wonderful meals they would prepare. We had our meeting on a sunny veranda in the rear of his home that overlooked the Mediterranean. He began to ask me questions about my life and with measured words I replied. I didn't know if he was sizing me up or what. In truth I had no idea why I was here other than I was kind of afraid not to. He must have noticed my apprehension and with a fatherly smile leaned forward and said I am not your enemy. If I had wanted to harm you we would not be speaking right now, as I'm sure you are well aware. I actually had hoped to help you learn more about business, and with your young mind perhaps I can learn from you as well. His wife walked in to invite us to our meal and now at least I would have a minute to convince myself whether I should believe him or not.

We walked into a medium sized room with simple fixtures, a large mahogany table, and thick sturdy chairs upholstered in very expensive looking black cloth. A platter of antipasto was already resting on the table, with a basket of fresh herb focaccia bread and a small glass pitcher of locally produced olive oil standing guard over it all. The room looked out over the water and as the smell of the food hit me I began to think I was in a dream. This was the most beautiful sight that I had ever seen. As far as I could see were nothing but villas, cliffs of marble, with wild flowers and trees mingled in between. The sunshine off the blue water was amazing and as I stood looking out the window Señora Bruno took my arm quietly, and very much like a mother guided me to my seat. She poured wine, although with respect to my age mine was shorter, and then began bringing in the primi, or first course of our lunch. She had roasted some fresh eggplant and summer squash with olive oil, local sea salt, and sprigs of fresh thyme picked from her own window box. Armando and I began to talk about our favorite food and I told him that growing up we had never had very much meat, so I really liked any kind but was very fond of beef, and particularly steak. He asked how I had it cooked and I smiled and said not very much. He laughed and said that for our meal next week he would ask his wife to get the biggest steak the butcher could cut, and then to cook it bloody rare!! I asked if I could not eat it all if I might bring the rest home for my brother and Sean to have. He leaned back and smiled like a man proud of his son. You look out for those who look out for you, he said. This is a Sicilian thing for sure, but in you I see it as pure as I have ever seen it in my life. I looked at him and said they would do the same for me, and he said than you are already a very lucky man, and at a very young age. Next came the secondi, or second course of linguine "pamo doro" with fire roasted roma tomatoes, fresh parsley, a pinch of red pepper and chopped garlic, and then finished with a flame of sweet marsala and a toss of grated Romano to melt slightly into the mix. As our meal progressed I began to feel more comfortable. I knew the food and the wine had that effect naturally, but my gut was telling me that he was alright. He talked to me about his childhood and learning how to move up the ranks in his family through brains and balls, but mainly brains. He explained how not everyone looks at things the way people like you and I do. He said that even at his age of 55 years, he still woke up every morning with a hunger in his eyes and a strength in his heart. He walked five miles and lifted weights every day as he no longer did any physical labor, but knew the value of maintaining a strong body along with the mind. He chuckled to himself and whispered and I still chase my bride.

Over the next months I visited at least once a week, and some weeks twice. Every time I learned more and more, and ate completely amazing food as well. I began to figure out that they had had two sons, but they were no longer with us. One had died in the war, and they didn't talk much about the other and I didn't pry. Armando explained how the different rackets and business ran and how to maintain maximum profits with minimal risk. He told me the biggest weapon I had was my eyes, for a skilled eye will see a small problem before it becomes a bigger problem and spins out of control. I said but what about the strength of your fists and your courage, and he said that while these had their place, the smartest men used their minds whenever possible, even when engaged in violence. He said a smart man can make enough money to hire someone else to enact his will for him, without having to ever even get out of his chair. He said as a young boy his father had always preached this to him, as his father had done with him, and his father before him. One day we were talking and I mentioned that I was getting a little tired of Arturo bothering me for just a little more. He was a degenerate gambler, and in spite of the fact that he kept us in the job that allowed us to pursue our other ventures I was getting sick of his shit. Don Bruno asked me if giving him a little more would keep any of us from enjoying the life we now had. I said no, but he is getting greedy and this is my problem with him. He suggested that I agree to give him a ten Lira per week increase, and another in six months. I did not understand this at first, so he explained. From what you have told me this man gives you the job that gets you out of the orphanage to make your extra money, and for this you reward him a very small amount of your profits. What if he fires you and your friends? What would you do then? At your age the monsignor still dictates the rules of your existence and without Arturo's help you would be back to stealing fruit yes? I agreed and he went on to explain that in reality what we were now giving to Arturo was in fact much less than other men in his position would have accepted. The Don said that his men would not even get out of bed for the amount that I paid Arturo, much less jeopardize their job, as he was doing for us every day. This now made much sense and I said so. The Don advised me to keep making my money, even raise the prices slightly to cover paying Arturo, but also to make sure that we always appreciated what we had for many people lose sight of this and this my friend will end your success quicker than anything else. Never forget Dominick "pigs get fat, but hogs get slaughtered."

Several months later one of the nuns approached me after dinner and said that I needed to come with her. Oh shit I thought, they found out about our business. She said nothing as we walked towards the infirmary and not the monsignor's office as I had thought we would. As we walked in the other nuns were busy tending to a young boy on a gurney with blood covering his swelling face and I asked the sister why we were here. She brought me into another room and said that Diamo had been attacked on his way home from the city and was beaten very badly. They did not know why but were attending to him. I realized now that my brother was the boy who we had seen on the gurney and I did not even recognize him from the severity of the beating he had taken. I stood to go to him and the sister insisted that I must stay with her for the moment, but that I could visit him later after they had tended to his needs and made sure he was okay. I began to feel my rage rise up and was visibly agitated. I asked if they knew who had done it and she explained that they didn't know much at all. A passing wagon had found him lying in the dirt, on the side of the road leading from the city to the orphanage, and we should thank God for this as he would not have lived through the night otherwise. We both crossed ourselves and said a small prayer of thanks, but my mind was already focused on retribution and not gratitude. In a few days the swelling began to come down and as Diamo regained consciousness he began to explain to me what he remembered, but said nothing to anyone else. He had been driving one of the orphanages horse and buggies back home with a small amount of our money, whiskey, and cigarettes along with the money he had made from selling the vegetables from the fields. I asked him why he was alone and he explained that it was a light day and Sean had stayed home. Arturo and his friends were drinking wine and talking to the girls in the plaza and had told him it was okay to ride home by himself. It was daylight and surely no one would harm a young boy driving a horse cart in the daylight. He explained that a man of about 20 had been walking along the dusty street and had waved him down to ask for a ride up the road to his village. Diamo, recognizing that it was a very hot day and a long walk, had agreed and allowed the man to jump up to ride beside him. They had only ridden for a few minutes and as they rounded a bend he saw three men standing in the middle of the road blocking their path. As he looked over at his passenger wondering how they should handle the situation one of the group approached the driver's side and said to get out. When he turned to face the stranger he felt a heavy object strike the back of his head and quickly fell to the ground. The three men, along with the man he had tried to help, quickly began hitting and kicking him. He lost consciousness soon after words and didn't remember anything else until waking up in the hospital. The thieves had taken everything, even the small notebook that my brother always kept, and disappeared, leaving my brother to die by himself on the side of a dirt road. I hugged him, and when I came back the next day handed him a fresh leather bound diary that I had purchased to replace the one the thieves stolen from him, and told him to just get better and not worry about any of it. I would handle it.

The next day I went directly to Don Bruno and in as calm a way as I could manage explained the situation and asked for his help. He told me it would take a little time, but he assured me he would find out who it was. For now we needed to go about our normal business for two reasons. I needed to keep our business operating, and we needed to not draw any attention from the local police. Diamo got better and from then on we always traveling with a minimum of three people in the wagon, and Armando gave us each a hand crafted stiletto that had been made from the strongest steel, with a black walnut handle and a thin leather pouch to carry it inside of our waistband at all times. The last thing I did every night before going to bed was to sharpen my knife with a small sharpening stone I had bought. I thought of the first blood it would taste and looked forward to that day with a calm enthusiasm. One afternoon the Don summoned me to his villa and said he had found out who it was and asked me if I would like his men to take care of it, or would I prefer to handle it personally. I said although I appreciated his help and his support, this was a job I wanted to myself. I didn't want to involve Diamo or Sean and would later find out that they were very mad that I hadn't. The following week I road with the Don and his bodyguard, with four of his soldiers following behind us in another truck, to a large barn far from the city. Inside were the bastards who had robbed and beaten my brother. They had been tied standing up to the large beams that supported the structure, and recognizing Don Bruno began visibly shaking and trying to protest their innocence through the black gag that had been tied around their mouths. He quietly explained to them that the man they had robbed was my brother and part of the money they had taken was intended to help feed orphans, and he spit on the ground. I noticed that one of them kept looking at me, even though he tried not to, and I knew this must have been the one who set it all up and was also probably the man who Diamo had tried to help. I told one of the soldiers to remove his gag and as soon as they did he began pleading for his life and blaming his friends for it all. The Don and I looked at each other, now knowing with certainty that this was indeed the man. One of the soldiers brought out a satchel which contained two pistols, a shotgun with a short barrel, an axe, and a thick wooden club. The Don asked me which I preferred and again offered the help of his men who each had a look in their eyes of cold anticipation. I produced the razor sharp stiletto from my waist band and said put the cloth back in his mouth. I walked up to the trembling assailant, looking up into his eyes and said I hope you die in as much pain as you gave to my brother. I stepped even closer to him, plunging the sharp steel blade into his stomach just below his navel and held my grip steady as he writhed in pain and tried to scream through the black cloth. I paused for a moment longer while maintaining both my grip and visual contact, then jerked the blade quickly upward. As I withdrew the stiletto his insides became exposed to the air and he screamed even louder as the men tied next to him began to piss in their pants. He would take a little while to die, and this suited me just fine. I stepped back, wiping the blood from my blade onto his shirt, and the Don asked about his co conspirators. I said he was the only one I wanted. Do with them as you please. I walked outside and lit up a cigarette, drawing the cool rich smoke into my lungs and smiling to myself with a satisfied thought of the revenge I had dealt out for my brother. A little while later the Don and his guard came out. We rode back to town leaving the soldiers to do their work and dispose of the bodies. When we reached his villa we went inside to sit on the back patio, looking out over the water and not saying anything. After a while he motioned for his wife to bring some grappa, coffee, and sweet biscotti she had prepared earlier. As the sun began to set we let the Italian liquor and dark coffee warm our insides and the Don said I will have my guard take you home. We have much to talk about. I thanked him for his help and thought about the day's events as we traveled back to the orphanage. As I got out of the carriage I thanked the driver, went upstairs, and slept better than I had in many weeks.

Seven

The next time I visited the Don we spent a great deal of time talking about the events of our past meeting. He asked if I had any questions or concerns about it, and I said my only concern is that the bodies are correctly taken care of. I didn't really feel like going to prison, particularly at the expense of someone else's lack of attention or disregard for the very real thought of the crime being discovered. The Don assured me with a confident look that his men were professionals and this was not their first time, so it was clean, start to finish. I didn't ask where they had been disposed of. I didn't need or want to know, and honestly I didn't care. He complimented me on both my prowess and calm efficiency and asked if this was my first time taking a life. I replied that it was not, but did not offer any more information. Good, he said, you also know when to speak and when to keep your mouth shut. With this combination we can find much work for you in the years to come. I told him that I wasn't looking for work per say as we were doing well with what we already had going, besides I said, both times it was personal. I don't know that I could do it for money. He leaned forward and looked at me with the most serious look I had ever been given and said Dominick, people who can do what you did can do it regardless of the circumstances, and those who cannot, cannot, it is that simple. Money really hasn't much to do with it other than making paying the bills a little easier at the end of the month. I thought about what he said for a while and agreed that inside it really had not bothered me. I didn't know if this was normal or not. It is what it is I guessed. I remember that prior to both of my removals I was much more anxious than during the actual act, and afterwards it left my mind completely within a few days. It wasn't that I was a sociopath or sick in the head, it was just that these people had been bad people and had hurt those that I loved. Revenge was simply as natural for me as breathing.

Don Bruno recognized talent, and he wasn't taking no for an answer, so I began to learn the trade at a very young age. We worked with knives at first. I was taught that this was the true test of your future and longevity in this business. Many people could pull a trigger, push a button, or run someone over with a car, but a true contractor had to have both the skill and confidence to get up close and personal if the job required it. One of my teachers said that when the day comes that you can remember the cologne of the man whose throat you just cut, then and only then will you be ready to move on. We traveled around Sicily, and even over to the mainland on occasion, for both training and low level street hits. The first several were just people who had maybe robbed someone or not paid their debts, but from the start I insisted on one rule; I would not kill women or children period and it was not nor never would be negotiable. My skill was becoming more obvious and my age allowed me to get closer to targets than other workers so the Don agreed to my terms. I voiced a concern over being gone from the orphanage so often and for so long and the Don just said not to worry about it. It has all been taken care of. I wanted to spend more time with Diamo and Sean, and especially Angelia as I missed her very much and didn't want some other boy to win her affections during my frequent absences. The Don addressed this as well and made it quite clear that not only where my brother and Sean now under his protection, but all the boys had been made aware that Angelia was now of limits and the price for violating this would be severe indeed. He had been occasionally sending her flowers and beautiful hand sewn dresses and scarves on my behalf to make up for my absence, but I knew that we both would prefer our time together over gifts, not that I didn't appreciate the gesture.

It was funny because I had begun to feel like a son to Armando more and more, and one day after work we sat once again looking over the water and preparing for the evening meal, and he turned in his chair to look at me and said Dominick I have begun to have a great trust in you. This is something very difficult for a man in my position, but I know in my heart that you would not betray me. You have the look of truth in your eyes and the strength of your word is clear with every word you speak. I was very honored and thanked him for both his support and friendship. He explained to me that his wife was also very fond of me and had concurred with the Don's opinion when they spoke about it prior to this night. He said they would like to adopt me and have me become their son. I was at a loss for words. Inside I was overcome with emotion but I didn't want to appear weak so I showed very little. The thought of having a father and a mother after all this time was very hard for me, and what about Diamo and Sean, and what about Angelia? Without us she would have no protection in the orphanage and I loved her. I could not abandon them regardless of what good things might lay in store for me. I brought this up, voicing my concern, and he asked if I thought they too would like to live with us. They had plenty of room, his wife loved to cook and they had never born a daughter which she had always longed for. Secretly I knew that they both missed their own boys very much and this was behind much of their reasoning, but I also trusted them and had been considering them as my family for many months now already. I said that I would speak to my brother and my friends, and when I returned to the orphanage that night I did.

Initially Diamo protested, and Sean followed suit I think just because Diamo did. Angelia said nothing, but she seemed to smile at the idea. The first thing he said was that we already had a family, us, and we didn't need anybody else. I let them both talk as

Armando had taught me, and then began to quash their objections one by one. I knew in my mind it was just the fear of change which everyone has, but I would still have to convince them to follow my decision. I had already made up my mind. I did not want to leave my brother, Sean, or Angelia, but I loved the Don and his wife and I knew without any question they both loved me like a son. I explained how this was really a once in a lifetime opportunity for us. We were all now in our teen years and teenagers did not get adopted. Everyone wanted babies and anyone in an orphanage new this. If you hadn't found parents by three or four, you weren't going to. I for one wanted a mom and a dad, even if it wasn't the ones who had given me life. The Bruno's were offering their home and their hearts out of love. They did not have to and they sure as hell didn't have to take in all four of us, but they would, and to me that meant a lot. It would mean we would all be safe all of the time. We would eat and be able to go to a doctor if we needed and not just some hack who was volunteering at the orphanage and clearly did not want to be there. We could go to real schools, and Diamo could go to college. We would be a real family.

Diamo said he wanted to think about it for the night and we all agreed. The next morning he explained that indeed he was a little bit apprehensive, but he knew I had always had our best interests in mind and he trusted my decisions, so he agreed. I was elated and could not wait to inform the Bruno's. I borrowed a horse and buggy from the stables with Arturo's ready approval, loaded up everybody and headed to the villa. When I told the Don I could see his chest swell with satisfaction while his wife had tears of happiness running down her tanned and gentle face. She disappeared into the cugina and returned with a small feast of cookies, biscuits, jams, coffee, and tea, as she ushered us all into the main eating room. While we dined on our treats she moved around the table like a women in a ballroom, tussling our hair as she passed by and kissing us individually on our foreheads with every pass. The Don sat quietly and I knew his heart was content at both the realization of having children once more in their home and the overwhelming joy that clearly engulfed his wife. Within the week all of the adoption paperwork had cleared. This normally took months but not for people like my father, and soon after our mother had four bedrooms of the house filled with new beds, new linen, beautiful hand carved furniture, and cabinets stocked with wonderful wool slacks and shirts for the boys, and pretty dresses of every color for Angelia. It was somewhat of an odd situation as Angelia and I were lovers, but our parents explained that it was their position that we had been in love well before being adopted, and we were not actually blood related so with a little discretion, and never in the home, our relationship could continue. As I said it was a little odd, but we all wanted to be together, so we made it work...

Eight

The next four years were the most wonderful of our lives. Father taught the boys more about business and honing our natural talents, while mother spent hour upon hour doting on Angelia, teaching her cooking skills and all of the other things a young Sicilian girl needs to know to become a women. I became more proficient in my trade, while Diamo spent most of his time studying and preparing to go to college. Sean loved the streets and the action so he pretty much took care of all aspects of our business with occasional help from me. Every night we would all have dinner together and talk about our days and what we had learned. Armando and his wife both glowed in the light of our energy and the love that we all had for one another and this felt so good to me. I had no way to thank them for all they had done for us, and we could never have repaid the debt, not that they would ever ask. I didn't speak about my work very much other than to occasionally mention the beauty or regional food we had enjoyed while off on our business. The Don kept everything in balance by supporting the deeds of the others, and showing the pride of a father to them all, while keeping our conversations more private.

No one had asked us to share our profits, but we all agreed to anyway. We were now so blessed that we all felt the need to repay their acts of kindness. Later we would find that the Don, while accepting our money with great appreciation had never spent one dime of it and would later give it back to us equally to help us in our future as adults. It eventually added up to a tidy sum.

When Diamo, Sean, and I were all around 16 we decided that we wanted to get a tattoo for each of us to signify our bond. We asked father about it and with some reservation he approved it. His only stipulations were that it be both small and placed in an area where no one could see it without us first revealing its existence. We decided on the upper left chest, as we always wore a shirt unless sleeping, and we decided on a very small song bird of simple design. We were all very fond of birds and had sat in the park or in the back of the orphanage listening to their pleasing songs and thinking about the freedom they possessed on many occasions. We visited a local man who did such work, making sure he knew who are father was and not to speak to anyone else about it. It would be our secret and for many reasons, some of which we would come to realize in later years. We visited him on a Saturday afternoon when he had no other clients and although it was slightly painful we were glad to have a now permanent bond between us. We had lived a very tough life until recent years and we never knew what the next day would bring, so having something that would never leave us, ever, meant a great deal.

We grew older and smarter, and Angelia and I began to speak of marriage and children someday. Diamo was trying to decide which university to attend. There were many choices in Europe, but the best medical schools were in America, and with a heavy heart he began to consider the possibility of leaving our beloved country for the first time. He didn't want to leave Sicily but more than that he did not want to leave us, and his heart already ached with the hurt he knew such a decision would bring to our mother and father. True to their character and love for us when the subject finally came up they were both supportive of both his decision and the wisdom behind it, although later that night I could hear mother quietly crying behind her bedroom door. In the next few days father had appeared to lose some of his vigor for life, but he explained it to us as just having a touch of the flu. We all knew better, but out of respect for his pride did not bring up the matter again. It was years away anyhow and there was no need to ruin the time we now had together with something that had yet to actually happen. The next year was fairly uneventful and life was normal and wonderful and then one day Angelia became sick. Mother tended to her for the first week, wiping her brow with cool clothes and keeping her with a constant cup of hot herb tea to chase off the illness, but she was getting worse. A local doctor came to the villa and began giving her strong medicine that we all knew would certainly make her better, but it didn't. She began to sleep more and more, and when she was awake could barely speak or even know who we were. I was really scared and did not know what to do. The Don sent for another doctor from Italy who was both very expensive and well renowned for his skill. In the end none of it mattered and Angelia died in her sleep on a Tuesday morning, at the age of seventeen. I felt like I had died with her and mother was not much better. I cried until I could not produce any more tears. Mother tried to go about her usual duties but with the look of a women who was now only a ghost herself. We buried her on a sunny autumn day with all of the people from our family and all of my father's business associates in attendance. My father's family had a private cemetery on the south side of our town overlooking the green blue sea. Angelia was buried in a handmade white silk dress with flowers and golden beads sewn into the fabric. The wind began to blow as they lowered her into the black earth and after everyone had left to return to town I found that I could not. I could not leave her. My love, the women who was going to bear my children and who I always knew I would grow old with, and she was now buried beneath the Sicilian soil. Later in the day father, Diamo, and Sean came to fetch me and with all of my strength now gone they quietly guided me to the waiting carriage.

The next months were very hard. We were all mourning the loss of our sister, daughter, lover and friend and mother was taking it the worst. I felt so bad for her and father. They had already lost their own children long ago and now had to go through it all over again. I wondered to the heavens how much pain and suffering one person should be expected to live through in their own life. Our adoptive parents had certainly had enough, and although we wanted and tried to ease the pain found that we could not. Father eventually regained much of his self but mother could not. This was the daughter she could never have had and I thought to myself if she would have been better off never having met Angelia or us in the first place. I felt very guilty about this for the longest time. I felt like it was my fault for bringing us all together and I could not lift the burden from my thoughts. My father was a very wise and intuitive man and one day while we were riding home from work asked me about my thoughts. I had been holding it all in for a long time and I unlike any other time in my life found that once I began speaking I could not stop. We pulled the carriage over under a shade tree on the side of the road and he listened to me for what seemed like hours. When I had said everything I had thought in the past few months he put his hand on my shoulder and said Dominick, none of this was your fault or ever within your control. God makes these decisions and man just has to live with them. Angelia got sick and she died. We all miss her greatly and it may seem unfair, but is not. People die in this world, and some before their time but that is just part of life and we must accept it. I said that I did not want to accept it. I wanted things to be like they were before, and as the first tear I had ever seen rolled down his face he said I know my son. I do too. In the year to come we talked about it on occasion and I found that this helped, and I think it helped him as well. Slowly life began to return and even mother was able to smile occasionally, which would make what was about to happen even harder.

We were now 18 and Diamo, who had worked very hard at his studies, had been accepted to the University of Michigan's medical school in the U.S. At the same time Sean was becoming more and more homesick for Ireland, and longed to return to his family once more.

Nine

The time had come and Sean had made up his mind to try his luck back in his homeland. The Don offered to at least purchase him a new identity and all the paper work to go with it, but Sean declined his offer saying he wasn't going to hide from the Dalcassians or anyone else. He would go back to start over and hoped to purchase his father's shop back from the current owner if it was still in business. We were all very sad to see him go but happy to know that he would be once again among his people. Sean was a proud man, and had been very thankful for everything done for him but now was the time to make his own family and make his own way. As he put it to me one night, if I'm going to be buried, which we all will someday I'd rather it be under the green fields of Ireland among my ancestors than anywhere else, and off he went.

He flew into Dublin and hitched a train south ward to Limerick city. The city hadn't changed much but Sean had. He left as a boy and now returned as a young man bearing no resemblance to his childhood years, but looking a wee bit like his grandfather. He didn't make a grand entrance when he got home figuring the smartest thing to do was get a feel for the city and the people once more. The Dalcassians as it turned out had heard about Sean's parents being killed. They hadn't known where the child had been ferried off to but were of the opinion that it was the old man who was a potential witness and not the son bearing his name so Sean was left alone. His father's shop had been sold and changed into a shoe repair place, which Sean knew absolutely nothing about, so he needed to come up with another way to make money. One day while sipping a pint in a local pub he was approached by a man much larger than him who the locals referred to as Mr. Wolfe. Sean was whistling a tune softly to himself as he watched a soccer game on the TV over the bar and waited for an order of cod and chips to arrive. The food was one of the things he appreciated most about being back in his own country. Pasta and wine were okay, but they were no substitute for bangers and mashed, or a good kidney pie piping hot from the oven. The man had whiskey on his breath and danger in his eyes as he told Sean you're in my seat. Sean paused briefly, taking another sip of his beer, and turned to the man asking is that so now, and standing up to face him. The stranger asked if he knew who he was and Sean replied no, and I don't really give a fuck either. There was a brief silence in the pub as the stranger sized up his challenger. If we're going to dance then let's have at it and may the best man win, if not you have two choices, you can sit down and join me for a pint, or you can fuck off. It doesn't really matter to me either way. The Wolf was certainly not expecting this from someone much smaller than him and in a pub where every single patron knew and feared him. He let out a big belly laugh and said damn if you aren't a true Irish son!! I would be honored to share a pint with the one lad in this god forsaken town who still carries a set of stones between his legs. The bartender quickly brought another pint, along with two shots of whiskey, and a new friendship was born.

Wolfe was a local leg breaker and on occasion hit man, so Sean and he had somewhat of a shared familiarity from the start. Limerick still had all of the vices it had when Sean left and had added a few more. Loan sharking, extortion, drugs, prostitution, and gambling where the big ones and there was always a need for someone to collect on a past due account or send a message that apparently wasn't quite clear. There was also a new crime family in town, and the competition provided plenty of cash. The McCabe's were just as dangerous as the Dalcassians and controlled the south side. They dabbled more in counterfeit goods and hijacking but maintained a substantial interest in the other rackets as well. As is true with any situation where competing powers operate in a small arena, the two groups randomly killed or injured each other over even the slightest of problems both real or imagined. When Sean and the Wolfe teamed up it was the perfect match. Sean was very smooth and could often get people to settle up, in part or in full, just based on the way he carried himself. On the rare occasion where someone jumped tough either Sean or the Wolfe would beat them within an inch of their life, and sometimes beyond it. Either way, the job got done and they got paid. One day a local night club owner who had been a bit of a celebrity on the rugby circuit back in the day, but now had an out of control gambling habit, decided to send a few guys after Mr. Wolf rather than pay his debt. This guy was a real prick and treated all of his employees like shit, especially the women. He used to pressure his waitresses into sex by making them give it up to him whenever he chose or risk losing their job, and jobs were very hard to find in Limerick city. He had hoped to send his own message I guess, but boy was he ever wrong. The Wolfe did a few days in the hospital but as soon as he got out he and Sean began plotting his revenge. The first thing they did was to steal the guy's one year old Mercedes 500 SEL. They parked it in a garage for a couple of weeks and then had it completely detailed, filled up the gas tank, and parked it back in front of its owners house with a note in an envelope taped to the windshield. When the owner came out the next morning he could not believe that his bright and shiny Mercedes was parked out front. He read the note which said; Dear Sir, I must apologize for the theft of your vehicle. I stole it away from you one night in the middle of a three-day drug induced binge. When I came about with a clear head I felt so ashamed that I had your car washed and waxed and filled up the gas tank. Please except this pair of tickets for the upcoming U2 show in Dublin as a further gesture of my remorse. The guy could not believe it (and shouldn't have) U2 tickets at the time were almost impossible to get and they were great seats to boot so the next weekend off to Dublin he went with one of the girls from the club. They had a grand time and when they returned to his home in a very wealthy part of the city found the place completely ransacked and vandalized with green paint. His safe was gone along with his many top shelf electronics, thousand dollar suits, a very large and expensive gun collection, and two kilos of uncut heroin that he kept in a spot he assumed was well hidden. He was raging mad and swore that whoever had done this would pay with their life even though he had never killed anyone before much less done any dirty work. He spent the next few nights drinking more than usual at his club and when he staggered out well after midnight he didn't notice the small brown package on the back floor board of his Mercedes. Unfortunately, the constable who pulled him over for suspicion of drunk driving did, and when he was whisked off to the local jail for a blood test and arraignment the next morning, the charge of distribution of a controlled substance would be added along with the drunk driving. It seemed that two things had happened. The club owner was an arrogant prick to just about everyone in town including the police who he had never so much as bought a round of drinks for in the past. This, combined with a phone tip received the night before had let to a situation where he wouldn't be bragging about his rugby career or making any bets for about the next five to ten years. He would however get very familiar with how it felt to be raped.

Sean and Wolfe went back about their business sharing pints and collecting money, and the world had returned to normal for the most part. One evening they were sitting in Flannigan's pub, which had long been regarded as a clean joint, when trouble once again came calling. By clean it meant that they didn't allow rough housing, dope dealing, or anything else. There were plenty of places in Limerick were you could get wild if that was you fancy but Flannigan's was not one of them and they planned to keep it that way. The owner's son Terry had run the front door ever since he became big enough to toss someone out and tonight he would prove his metal once again. Johnny McCabe had a reputation as both a fighter and a dealer, and Terry Flannigan knew him well. When the young McCabe decided to have a go at Flannigan's he was immediately stopped at the door. What the fuck is your problem. Is my money not just as green as the next man's Terry? The doorman wasn't looking for trouble, but he knew that if he let the man in trouble is exactly what would follow. There are plenty of other pubs in Limerick where you can have your fun Mr. McCabe this just isn't one of them. Looking at the two rough looking street soldiers standing behind their now angry friend he figured he better be ready to fight and right quick. You fucking Irish prick, who are you to tell me where I can and can't go, now get the fuck out of me way or you'll see what's what!!

The doorman held his ground saying nothing and the challenger knew that even with his back up he would not beat Flannigan in a fight and Terry had back up too. So that's the way we are eh? Mr. Terry Flannigan thinks he's going to disrespect me in my own city then? We'll just see about that, and off they went. Sean and Wolfe weren't there two nights later when two men, their faces wrapped in balaclavas, walked in the front door and without a word shot Terry Flannigan seven times in the chest. Every one inside the pub scattered as the gunman fled, everyone that is but Megan McCabe, who rushed to the side of her now dead lover as he bled out on the worn wooden floor. People in Limerick city knew enough not to talk. Common sense dictated that you would live much longer if you kept quiet and the local crime families kept this rule fresh in the minds of everyone in town, and had never sustained a single criminal conviction because of it. Megan would be the first one to break the rule.

he knew what her family did, and she knew her brother had ordered the hit but she was justifiably scared to open her mouth. Her brother Johnny was big in the drug business and very successful at his trade. He had ordered a brand new Lincoln SUV from the U.S. just six months previous and this thing was decked out to the nines. It had a custom leather interior, a hand carved wooden dash, $3,000 stereo, diamond plate trim and running boards, and was completely bulletproof. It was a dandy, that's for sure, and the only one in all of Ireland.

Johnny headed to Dublin one day to pick up his new truck and a load of ecstasy when on the way back he was stopped by the local police. The officer was mainly curious to see who was driving such a fancy vehicle but when he identified the driver he knew a search of the vehicle was most definitely in order. They easily discovered the drugs confiscating both the dope and the vehicle as the young McCabe laughed and said don't scratch it. You'll be returning it to me soon enough. He would have probably been right as his attorney argued that being a brand new vehicle, fresh off the ship, someone else had hidden the drugs and not his client. What the arrogant young man did not realize was at that very same moment his sister had decided she could no longer keep quiet, and was giving a statement to the local magistrate about her brother ordering the killing of Terry Flannigan. Father McCabe told everyone to stay calm. When his daughter came home he would either talk or beat some sense into her. Either way it was no problem. She would not be going to court of this he was quite sure. The young girl had thought about her fate long before she ever entered the police station. She knew a few things; she could never go back. She no longer wanted to, and her brother had killed the only man she ever loved.

Her father was furious, partially over being kept from speaking to his daughter, but mainly over her turning on a family member. Her own brother for fucks sake, what was she thinking? He tried to get a note to her, not sure if she ever received it. Whether she had or not he got no response. He was interviewed by a local TV station and like a wolf in sheep's clothing shed a tear on camera as he pleaded for his daughter to come home, and still no response. As the months went by he began to lose hope that he could ever persuade the now police-protected women to change her mind. Mean while his young son sat in jail, his reputation was beginning to suffer, and still the armor plated SUV remained locked up; the only one in all of Ireland.

Old man McCabe had enjoyed a long running fight with the local police chief. They had been playing cat and mouse long before either one had gotten good at their respective occupations. McCabe kept busy, and got bigger, and still the police could never catch him. When on occasion they would meet on the streets the crime boss would simply smile and tip his hat. The cop never smiled, or tipped his hat, although he did use one of his fingers for another form of acknowledgement. Now the boss was worried. He still could not understand his daughter infidelity, and over a fucking Flannigan on top of it. His wife occasionally asked when Megan would be coming home, and he always offered the same response; soon my darling, very soon.

Two weeks before the trial it had become clear that the young women was sticking to her word, and with the hardest decision he would ever make upon him, old man McCabe picked up the phone. The voice on the other end was a well regarded sniper with plenty of experience, and no reservations. When they met in person the situation was spelled out, a plan was made, and money changed hands. The contractor assured him that it could be done, asking the old man once more if this was indeed his choice. With an ice cold stare he confirmed his request, and the plan was set in motion. The witness would be brought to the rear of the court, just like those before her. They would pull up close to the door which had concrete walls on both sides, and a steel awning overhead that protruded out to create a situation where the persons exiting the vehicle would be blocked from both sight and harm by the cement barriers and the protective metal overhead. Unfortunately for the occupants anyone with a high powered rifle could easily see and shoot the occupants well before they ever exited the vehicle, but since this wasn't a very busy court the shooter knew that no one had ever considered this.

On the day the trial was supposed to begin the assassin sat comfortably in a second story room across the alley that he had prepared a week ahead. He was positioned back four feet from the window so the police would never know where the shot had come from, and he knew that he would only need one anyway. He was waiting patiently, going over the shot in his head; if it was a sedan he would focus on the rear window for his profile, if it was a van he would line up through the side, either way he had a titanium tipped 308 that would surely guarantee the young women's silence in the next few minutes, and he lit up a Chesterfield to kill the time. As he put out the cigarette the shiny black vehicle pulled up right where he expected. It wasn't a sedan or a van but the situation was the same as he observed the young women's profile through the side rear window. He lined up the shot, slowed his breathing almost to a stop, and gently squeezed the trigger. What happened next challenged both his mind and his eyes. The bullet that should have easily penetrated the glass, had simply stopped as if in mid air. The window of the vehicle looked like a spider's web on a sheet of ice, but was still most definitely intact. As he quickly chambered another round the door of the room exploded inward and as he turned a burst from a submachine gun lifted him off his chair and his rifle fell to the ground.

In the alley below two squads of Irish soldiers had come out of their hiding places and had now surrounded the still very intact bullet proof SUV, the only one in all of Ireland.

With the new revelation, Megan decided that she had even more information to share and her father and all of her brothers now sat glaring in their jail house clothing. The trial didn't take long. The people of Limerick and the local police had been increasingly tired of the local crime in years past, any easily convicted the accused on all counts. Sean and the Wolfe sat at the bar watching the verdict on local television while sipping on a pint.

When their food arrived Wolfe asked his friend to pass the salt as he said you know this is going to affect our business, and I'm damn sick of the rain and the cold. Perhaps it's time for a warmer place to call home.

———————————————

Ten

Diamo had accepted the university's offer and I knew that as hard as it would be for me to leave Sicily and our adoptive parents I could not leave my brother and must follow him to America. I knew it must once again have been very hard for Armando and his wife, but true to their undying love for us, they both understood our decision and offered their unwavering support. The Don was able to spread some money around which expedited the process a great deal. Diamo was expected to begin classes in the fall so on a hot July day we boarded the plane for America and our new home. Mother had packed us a lunch for the trip with home baked bread, prosciutto and capocolla, farmers cheese, calamata olives picked from our orchard, homemade preserves, cannoli that she had filled that morning, and two small clay bottles of her homemade plum brandy, which, while much stronger than the store bought kind, was perfectly fine for us as we were used to drinking it. Two of the stewardess's on the trip over commented on our bountiful feast and we offered to share both our food and drink with them, as was common courtesy in our country. They both laughed and politely declined but allowed us to get to know them much more intimately upon our arrival in the U.S. If this was the way that people treated you in America we both agreed that we would enjoy it very much.

The University of Michigan was in Ann Arbor, Michigan and after arrival we quickly began searching for a house to buy that would be convenient for Diamo's classes. The first few people we spoke with must have assumed that as two men not yet 20 years of age, we surely could not be serious about buying a home, particularly one near to campus as they were very expensive. We were both quite surprised at this response as in Sicily people were made well aware at a very young age that when it came to money we were both amply supplied, and quite serious. It actually worked out in our favor for when we found a home that we both agreed we liked, negotiations were viewed with an air of humor on the part of the realtors. When we offered them $20,000 less than they were asking, in cash, and backed up our offer with a letter from the local bank guaranteeing our ability to pay a sum much higher, they were no longer laughing. They accepted our offer after a slight counter offer and we moved in and quickly furnished the home with what we needed. The next step was getting drivers licenses and purchasing an automobile, as Americans did not use horses or carts. We settled on a three year old car with four doors and a very nice radio, as we both loved music. Father as I said had saved all of the money we had offered him, and although he had given one third to Sean when he left there was still plenty left over for our needs. I knew if we had needed his help additionally he would have gladly offered it, but between the amount he had save for us (and we both agreed he had added some of his own), the money we had saved over the years, and the gold coins that I had kept hidden for all of these years and recently sold, we came to the U.S. with a little over $300,000 between us. We were a little nervous being in a new country, but the one thing we were not concerned with in the least was money.

Diamo began his classes and I knew very quickly that this would consume much of his time for the next few years, so I began to study the area for a potential business idea to begin. Father had both associates and distant relations in Detroit and Chicago, and I realized that I would be expected to occasionally ply my former trade, but I also needed something to do in my spare time. The college town had a ton of restaurants, and a few sandwich shops they called delis but no true Italian food. Diamo suggested opening my restaurant as I had always talked about but I knew from watching the restaurateurs in Sicily that a full scale establishment was a ton of work and I simply would not have the time. I noticed that the places that sold sandwiches were always busy, made very good money from putting together bread, meat, and cheese, and were absolutely crazy on football Saturdays, but were only open for lunch and limited dinner hours, and were always closed on Sundays. I tried a few of their sandwiches and some places version of an Italian sandwich, which I took two bites of and promptly gave the rest to an unchained dog out front. I found a small place that had formerly been a deli but had been closed down for some reason. I thought about buying the building but commercial real estate was much more expensive than residential, and I did not know how long I would want to make sandwiches. The man wanted $1,300 a month for rent, plus utilities, and I thought this was very high, especially compared to our old town. I had been researching rents in the area and although he was a little high, he wasn't that far away from what other people were getting. I knew offering to pay the first year up front would probably save me a couple thousand, but again I was not sure if this would be something I would be doing for any length of time, so I offered him $1,000 a month and agreed to a $100 per month increase the following year, but no more for the next two, and he agreed. It took me a while to figure out what equipment I would need and where to get a supply of good quality Italian meats and cheeses that I was adamant about using in our products. I knew that I would be also eating what I served my customers, and I was not eating bad food no matter how much it saved us in costs. I ended up finding a Jew run supplier in Detroit, and although they were not Italians they were the only place fairly local that could provide a good Italian product, and not fuck you on the price. They had excellent ham, braesola, capocolla, and prosciutto, with three different choices of provolone and a very good fresh mozzarella that I would use in our salads. The only thing I couldn't get from them was decent olive oil and roasted peppers, but I found another place not far away that was pretty close to what we were used to. I went on the computer and while trying to come up with a name found a place in Manhattan New York called *Steve's Hero's and Hoagies*. I found out that a hero sandwich or submarine was the American name for the Italian cold sandwiches that my mother had occasionally prepared for us when we were traveling or simply did not feel like cooking a lunch meal. We never complained as they were both delicious and filling. She would start with a whole loaf of fresh baked semolina bread, which she would first cut down the middle, spooning a mixture of olive oil, salt, pepper, and dried oregano and basil on both sides. She would then layer it with at least three different meats, and either provolone or fresh mozzarella, topping it off with fresh chopped roma tomato, a few slices of sweet onion, and then a splash of red wine vinegar. She would wrap it in paper and tie it with a piece of brown twine to make it safe to transport and eat later in the day. When you opened it all of the flavors had blended and it was quite amazing to eat.

I called my shop "Hero's Submarines" and began selling real Italian sandwiches, exactly like my mother had made for us to the hungry student population. We became very successful almost overnight and I was able to both make plenty of money and meet plenty of college girls. They liked a few more toppings then we have put on in Italy. Lettuce and mayonnaise, I could never understand either of these on a sandwich but I figured they were paying for it so who gives a shit and gave them what they ask for. One weekend I made up a batch real meatballs like we had in Sicily with homemade marinara sauce to top it with. I was going to serve it over pasta for lunches the coming week, but the staff told me that meatball subs were very popular so that's what we did. I had to leave early that day to take care of some business. When I got back my manager told me that we had sold out of them and people were asking for more. I told him he was mistaken and to look in the walk in cooler. I had made up a 100 pounds of meatballs along with 10 gallons of sauce. There was no way in hell we went through all of it in one day, especially a Monday. He told me that he had taken them out to refill our warming pots half way through the lunch hour, but we had sold all of those as well. We soon began making and selling 200 and some weeks 300 pounds of homemade meatball subs alone. I didn't think I would enjoy it as much as I did but found that particularly at its craziest times it was a an absolute riot!! I loved being around people and made quick friends with many of my customers. I also began learning a lot about American music, particularly rock, reggae, and rhythms and blues, and during our lunch would play a wide variety that the customers all seemed to really enjoy as much as we did. I would occasionally throw in some of Italian ballads from the old country, and while no one complained they clearly preferred the other stuff, so I began to play it only during the slower times when things were settling down.

Eleven

It was early spring and business was great. I loved our new home and our new country and liked to sit outside at night when I got home from a busy day to listen to the sounds of the always vibrant college town. Our house sat on a slight hillside overlooking Ann Arbor and the neighbors below us. We decided to build a big deck off the back to entertain and eat our evening meals. We put in a Jacuzzi and a very nice wood fired grill of brick and mortar, with an oven for making pizza on stones like we did back home. It was very pleasant when the sun went down and many times I would just sit quietly and listen to the sounds of the night, until one night I heard the quiet cries of a young girl on the porch of the house that lay below ours.

I figured it was probably just one of the many things that upset young women, so I left it alone, but when it began happening more frequently I found that I could no longer ignore it. One day when I heard her crying to herself in the dark again I walked down the hill and close enough to the fence that separated our yards to say hello in a quiet voice. She stopped crying and I had obviously startled her, but I explained that I was only her neighbor and had been concerned about her from hearing the sound of her sobs. She thanked me, but did not approach, and said it was okay, and walked back into her house. I waited another week, still hearing her cries in the darkness every other night, and then decided to speak with her parents. I thought that maybe she was just sad, possibly mentally ill, or maybe had broken up with a boyfriend recently. When I knocked on their door the next afternoon the step father answered and made it very clear he was not a fan of intrusion. He was dressed in an old Harley Davidson t-shirt, with tattered jeans, a face that had not been shaved in days, and the odor of diesel and a lack of bathing. I introduced myself as a neighbor and told him about what I had heard in evenings past. I don't know if it was my age, my accent, or my skin color, but he told me he didn't give a fuck who I was and to mind my own business, the old wooden door slamming quickly in my face. My first thought was he's right, it's not my business or concern, but I guessed the girl to be maybe 13 or so, and something was obviously wrong. With my life in the orphanage still very real in my memory, I simply could not ignore it. I began to get a feeling like when I was watching someone before a job, and I allowed my natural ability to take over. Hero's was running smoothly so I started spending more time observing their home and listening at night. I purchased a pair of very good compact binoculars, along with a couple of sets of small radio transmitted listening devices from a surveillance company online. I followed the step dad a few times and did it again when they would go out as a family, easily beginning to put together their routines. They didn't do much but would occasionally take in a movie at a local theater, or go to one of those all you can eat buffets that Americans were so fond of. One Wednesday evening when I knew they were going to be out for a while I slipped in through an old window with a crappy lock in the back of their house. Once inside I made my way efficiently through the home, placing the listening devices strategically in the rooms where I knew I could gain the most Intel. I found a desk and a small lock box which I easily opened, finding information inside that further enhanced what I already knew about them and how they lived. I slipped out the window again satisfied with my knew information, and went back up to our deck eagerly awaiting their return and the chance to test out my gear. Two hours later they returned and began feeding me immediately with what I wanted. Within a week I had surmised that the step father was basically a factory rat drunk and a low level coke dealer, who spent every night after work drinking, snorting, or smoking weed. The mom was a Jerry Springer rerun addict with a penchant for cheap vodka and bad hairdos, and a face you could use to make gorilla cookies. I wondered how people like them could have afforded a house in this area even though it was now quite run down. I came to find out that Ginny, the mom, had inherited it from her grandmother who was apparently fond of her in her younger years and had left her the house along with a little cash, which was all long gone. The step dad Billy had come along just before and took over as both husband and father, quickly putting his own stamp on the mom and step daughter. After a few more weeks I would finally find out where the young girls tears were coming from.

It was late summer and in our neighborhood most people left the windows open at night to allow the cool night air to enter their homes. I could hear easily with the devices, and what I heard on the receiver was now reinforced with the partnership of the quiet night air and the open windows. One evening after dark I was listening in on their activity, and I could tell that Billy was in rip roaring form as usual. Ginny had announced she was going to bed and a short time later I heard the daughter Rachel ask her step father to leave her alone. It was obvious from the conversation that he was not going to, and after the sounds of his grunts and groans had subsided I could hear her quietly crying once more in the darkness of her small bedroom. Motherfucker I thought to myself. Of all the possibilities I had considered, this was not one of them. I was so dumbstruck by the revelation it was all I could do not to walk right down the hill, slip in through the window again, and cut his fucking throat. I couldn't sleep the entire night and now allowed all of my experience to guide my thoughts for his much needed demise. I could just clip him. It would be easy enough. I could hit him on his piece of shit motorcycle on the way home from work but it would be too messy and there would most certainly be witnesses. I could break into the house as night when he was fucked up and just shoot him and make it look like a dope robbery, but again this would be too messy and Rachel might see or hear it. It also left Ginny as a variable, and as much as I wanted to break them I had my rules. Then it came to me...

I had a customer at Hero's who was an insurance salesman and had been bugging me for months to buy a policy. I had always politely declined, but now asked him for his advice on an insurance matter. I told him I had a friend with a drug problem, and I was concerned for his families survival after what I was certain would be his inevitable end from the habits of his life. I wanted to know what the requirements to establish a policy for his family would be. Did I have to get him to actually come in and sign the document as I knew he would not or could I just pay for the policy, bring it to him and have him sign off on it. He told me that as long as I could get a verifiable signature that I could in fact just pay for it and he would activate it. The only advice he gave was not to be extreme with the amount of the policy. Insurance companies weren't stupid and liked paying out money about as much as anyone else did. I asked him what he would suggest and he said as long as you don't go over $250,000 you won't have a problem. I thanked him for his valuable advice and assured him I would be in touch soon. The next day I knocked on the door of the neighbors once more and Billy answered as usual. He gave me a dirty what the fuck do you want look, that is until he recognized the case of Wild Turkey whiskey I held under my arm. Wild Turkey, as I already knew, was his drink of choice. He said what you got there and I explained how I had a business friend who had connected with a disgruntled trucker from a local liquor distributorship and had bought a few cases of booze for 40 cents on the dollar. I explained that I didn't drink whiskey and wondered if he did or knew of anyone else who might be interested. This was like taking candy from a baby, and as the white trash piece of garbage's eyes lit up he exclaimed brother you just knocked on the right door, WT is my drink!! He told me to come in and yelled at Ginny hey babe get in her, Christmas came early this year! What did you say your name was again and reached out to eagerly shake my hand. Ginny came in and was unimpressed with the booze, as I said she was a vodka drinker. She sized me up though and gave me a sort of slippery reptile like smile, unbeknownst to her husband. He paid me for the stuff and invited me to stay for a drink. I said I couldn't. I didn't want to be too easy, and he said they were watching the game on Saturday and barbequing, come on over and have some chow with us and bring some more booze if you got it. I didn't know what chow was but said I would try. He pumped my hand once more, thanked me for the whiskey, and said come on over anytime neighbor, anytime...

I showed up on Saturday and faked appreciation as I slowly ingested Ginny's horrible cooking. I had actually become a fan of American barbeque, but this crap was just some over cooked garbage, doused in store bought sauce and was nothing like the stuff I was used to. I kept my drink watered down and Billy kept wanted to refill it, luckily they had a planter next to my chair and in their inebriated stated never noticed me watering the plant. I laughed at his jokes all the time wanting to end this shit and get back to my life but I needed to help the girl so I just shut up and smiled. I visited frequently over the next few weeks and noticed that Rachel rarely came out of her room except when her parents demanded that she clean the kitchen or act in others ways like an indentured servant. One night when they were both really fucked up Billy asked me what I thought of his daughter. I said I didn't really know what he meant and he asked if I thought she was hot. I was without words and he continued to say hey she's young, but she's prime pussy brother, with his wife simply watching TV, incoherent to our conversation or so I thought. I don't know I said, playing along, I guess she's pretty. Billy said well if you ever want to get with her all you have to do is say so. I tap that ass on a regular basis, but I don't mind sharing with a friend, to which Ginny turned and said Billy you are so bad... Wait a second I thought, her mom even knows about the step dad fucking her kid? I've had some moments in my life that required an extreme amount of self control, but this was in a whole other universe. As I clinked glasses with him I said appreciate the offer bro, maybe someday I'll take you up on it, and we all went back to watching the game. I went home that night full of a rage and disgust that I could not even get my mind around. I'm a Sicilian, and we're well known for our passion and our temper, but this, oh my God, this was simply vile. I had so many thoughts on how to kill him, and after very little reflection included Ginny in the package. I didn't do women or kids, but I was breaking the rules. This bitch had to go. The next day I picked up the application for insurance.

I knew Billy would never sign it, but I also had a side hobby of forgery and was quite good at it. On my next visit for drinks I excused myself to use the bathroom and quickly rummaged the desk for something with his signature on it. Within a couple of days I had it down perfectly and placed a fake signature on the paperwork that I knew would hold up to any investigation. I made Rachel the beneficiary and paid the first six months premium up front on a policy for $200,000. I had to wait a little bit. As much as it pissed me off to do so, I knew I simply could not get an insurance policy on somebody and kill them a week later. I needed to get Rachel out of the house for the night and persuaded the sister of one of my employees who was a friend of hers to get her to go watch a local band that would keep her busy for at least a few hours while I did my work. The night I decided to finish it I brought a handful of Quaaludes to help me out. Lemmon 714's were easy to come by in a college town and I knew that it wouldn't be too difficult to slip them into Ginny and Billy's drinks once we were partying. We ordered a pizza, poured some drinks, and popped *Reservoir Dogs* into the DVD player. The pizza arrived and just before Ginny refilled everyone's glass I popped a couple of crushed up ludes into both of their drinks and sat back waiting for the drugs to take effect. I didn't have to wait long. Billy was a pretty big dude, and had a tolerance already for dope but he was used to weed and blow and not Quaaludes. After about an hour I could see a smile start to spread across his dirty face, Ginny just sat in her chair with an increasingly stupid look, suddenly announcing that she was tired and was going to bed. I had brought a couple of cigars and asked Billy if he would like one. With slurred speech he said sure as I lit it up for him. I watched him toke on it for a few minutes, and then all of the stuff he had ingested came calling. His head rolled back onto the easy chair and a moment later the lit cigar dropped to the worn carpet. I picked it up, temporarily placing it in the ashtray next to him, and went to check on the wife. As I walked into their bedroom she was still awake and wearing only a pair of cheap thong panties from Wal-Mart. She looked up at me and asked were Billy was. I said he had passed out already and asked her if she wanted some action now that her old man was incognito. She smirked and said I wondered how long it was going to take you to come around Dominick as she reached for my belt buckle. I took her hand away and said I wanted to fuck her from behind as her eyes lit up and she easily rolled over onto her stomach. I put my hand on her shoulder and as she awaited what she thought would be my sexual desires, punched her right in the base of the skull. I knew that with this and the drugs she wouldn't be waking up any time soon, and I headed back to the living room to prepare for finishing the job. They weren't much on housekeeping and I easily found an ample supply of old magazines and other flammable items. I filled a waste basket with paper and tissues, placing it next to Billy's chair, and then piled stacks of other combustible items directly around it as if it had simply accumulated from laziness on their part. I put a fan in the window three feet from his chair and turned it on medium speed as I blew on the smoking cigar to brighten the ember. The house had so much shit in it I knew that once the waste basket caught fire from the burning cigar I was about to drop into it, aided by the oxygen that the fan would supply, the house and its contents would catch fire with relative ease. I let myself out the back door and went to wait on my deck as the fire took hold.

Within a half hour I could see a clear fire raging in the living room and no one had exited the home. When the fire trucks finally arrived the most they could hope for was to keep the fire from reaching the other homes around it. The home itself would end up a big pile of rubble, and the world would be a little better place. I was out front when Rachel and her friend arrived and she asked what had happened. I said I didn't know but that it would all be okay, not letting on that I was fully aware of what had just left her life. In the weeks that followed Rachel's aunt would step in to offer her a place to live. The funeral was without incident and with the well known lifestyle that Billy and Ginny had not only enjoyed but flaunted, there would be only a superficial investigation, during which it would be determined that the blaze had started in the living room from Billy falling asleep while smoking in his favorite chair. Ginny actually died from smoke inhalation, but toxicology reports would reveal that both had large amounts of various narcotics in their systems which clearly demonstrated a history of drug abuse. Rachel would get counseling, and eventually go to college. She had no difficulty paying for either, as she had received $200,000 from a life insurance policy that she never knew existed...

———————————————

Twelve

I had been asked to take care of some business in Chicago for one of my father's associates, so after a two and a half hour drive I found myself stopped at a red light in a pretty rough area on the south side of shy town. I had my window rolled down and a black dude standing on the corner looked in my direction, took off his shades, and said you're in the wrong neighborhood white boy. I smiled and said thanks as I drove off. I went to meet with Gino, the man ordering the work, and he explained to me how the target in question was some big black dude that ran a pawn shop and had been a regular distributor for the mob run heroin business for quite some time now. The problem was that the guy had started being later and later on his payments in recent months until one week he just decided not to pay at all. Apparently he had also been peppering the streets with some pretty cocky remarks about his position, versus that of his suppliers. This is what really made Gino mad. The money was one thing, but protecting your reputation was equally important if not more, and this dude was making Gino look bad. He told me a little of what he had heard and laughingly said I guess this fucking eggplant thinks he's that brother in New Jack City or some shit. He made it very clear that he wanted the record set straight and he wanted people in the area to hear the message loud and clear.

After our meeting I made a few passes by the pawn shop easily deciding to seek lodging elsewhere for the night. When I got up the next day I drove by the shop looking for entrances and exits, and calculating pedestrian traffic flow. I parked my car a block away and quickly changed into my disguise. I had purchased an oversized pair of work slacks, oversized and weathered army jacket, a Chicago Cubs baseball cap, and a pair of basic but inexpensive sunglasses that morning at a thrift shop a few miles away. I smeared some grey camouflage face paint on my cheek bones and forehead to make my face seem tired and a bit older and began to walk towards the shop, looking for cameras and taking in the hours and days of operation. I briefly walked around to the back alley looking more like a homeless vet than a hit man. I had a gun on me but I sure as hell didn't want either problems or someone remembering me so I kept it real cool. I saw one camera that I could tell was too old to be still functioning, and a brand new Lincoln with chrome rims parked inside of the locked and fenced in rear of the place. I made my way back to my car committing to memory a mental map of both the building and its surroundings and decided to go find some lunch.

After driving for about ten minutes I saw a sign that read Soul Queen home cooked soul food, best in Chicago!! I didn't believe it was the best as Chicago had a ton of great restaurants from every variety but it looked decent, so in to the parking lot I pulled. I was the only white dude in the place and for a brief moment people were staring when the hostess or whatever she was walked up and said can I help you sugar? I said yes I'm hungry, and lying, said that a friend had told me that this was in fact the best soul food restaurant in town. She said your friend didn't lie, but you sure you know where you're at? Ain't a lot of white folks around here. I said it's cool with me if it's cool with you, and she said yeah, I'm cool, just so long as your money is green baby, and we don't take checks and we don't take plastic. We both smiled as she showed me to a booth. I looked over the menu and honestly wanted one of everything except chitterlings. I was always up for new food experiences but I didn't eat anything that came anywhere near to an animal's asshole, cock, or balls. The waitress brought me some sweet tea and homemade cornbread and asked what I wanted. I settled on the down home sampler with spare ribs, catfish fried in cornmeal, turnip greens, macaroni and cheese, candied yams, and a piece of pecan pie for dessert. When my food arrived I was in heaven. Everything was made from scratch and you could tell with every bite that whoever made it actually gave a damn about pleasing their customers. After lunch a short black man came walking by my table to ask how my meal was. I'm always enthusiastic about good food, and this was no exception as I generously ladled out my compliments to the chef. He said that this was his place and that he was glad to hear I had enjoyed my lunch. I was half expecting him to be now the third person in 24 hours to comment on my skin color but he just wiped his hand on his apron, sticking it out to shake mine, and said Sidney Rawls nice to meet you. We chatted for a little longer and he asked what business I was in. I said that it wasn't the kind you talked about. He smiled again, said that's cool brother and excused himself to get back to work. After I left I stopped by a hardware store and paid cash for a roll of duct tape and a pair of heavy duty bolt cutters. Next I stopped by a sporting goods place outside the city limits and purchased a 22 caliber pellet gun.

I spent the next couple of days watching the pawn shop for a while, checking out new places for lunch, and then going back at closing time to monitor the owner's routine for closing up. I would have loved to have eaten at Soul Queen for every meal but that would make it way to easy for someone to remember me, so I couldn't do it. The fourth night I went to the back alley 20 minutes before they closed and using the pellet gun shot out the two flood lights with only the noise of the cracking glass from the tiny hole the pellet had made. I cut the chain on the fence and easily made my way up to the side of the rear entrance as I waited for show time. At exactly 9:15 the door opened and a big muscular looking brother stepped out, turning with his back to me to lock up. I quietly stepped to his side and said back inside and don't try any funny shit or you're a dead man. With my pistol to the back of his head he readily complied and when we were inside with the door now shut I said now, shut off the alarm and don't enter a panic code or mine will be the last voice you ever hear. He complied as fast as his nervous fingers could punch the buttons and as soon as the green light came on I shot him in the back of his upper right leg with the silenced 38. He grabbed his leg turning and stumbling into a storage shelf as he looked at me in agony and said what the fuck did you do that for? Take the money and get your ass out of here, goddamn!! Terence was about six four and came in at well over 300 pounds. I looked him right in the eye and said I shot you so you would know I wasn't some punk fucking around. Now where's the safe? I threw him the roll of duck tape and told him to tape his leg so he didn't bleed out, which he quickly did. I then had him turn his back to me as I took the roll and duct taped his left hand securely around the back of his waist. He was strong, but this is a trick that I had used in the past as it's very hard to free your arm and I could easily shoot him well before he could present any real threat any-how. I had been watching him and knew he was right handed, so he would still be able to open the safe. We went to the office and first I pulled out the DVDs that he used for recording from the existing surveillance cameras and then I asked him where the other recorder was. There's always a hidden one if they know what they're doing, you just have to look. He said that was all he had and I pointed the gun at his balls and he freaked out saying damn motherfucker are you crazy! I jammed the gun into his crotch and he quickly told me where the other recorder was hidden in a cupboard above the coffee pot. Once I got him to open the safe I explained to him that I was not in fact a robber, but a person hired by the people he had owed 50 grand too and was refusing to pay. He might have got off with a warning but being an ex-college football player with a big ego and a bigger mouth he had been overheard telling the locals that he wasn't paying those wop mutha- fuckers shit and he dared Gino to bring his punk ass into his neighborhood. Big mistake dude, big mistake...

He said that he would pay and that we could work it all out. He had a lot of connections and could make us a lot of cash if we let him. What he failed to understand was that my job was not in negotiations. The time for that was well past and he had proved to be a liability already so I put two rounds into his chest and walked behind him, now on the ground, to put two more into the back of his head. I emptied the safe which had around 70 grand in cash and a bunch of gold jewelry wrapped up in cloth. I had been wearing gloves so there was no need to wipe anything off, and I packed the goods into a briefcase from his office. I went to the front, unlocking the front door, and switched the open sign back on. I knew that in this rough of a neighborhood the first person to walk in the door the next day would figure out that no one was home, and the store's inventory would quickly find its way back onto the streets it had came from. They might find Terence, I'm sure someone would, but by then it wouldn't really matter. So many people would have walked through the place by that point that the crime scene would be completely compromised. Not that the local cops gave a damn anyway. I'm sure they knew about the heroin dealing and to them it was just one more dealer off the streets, with a hundred more waiting to take his place the next day. I walked out of the back of the building and slowly made my way back to my rental car so as not to attract attention. The next morning I brought 50 grand to the Gino, who paid me, thanked me, and offered to show me the finer parts of Chicago. I said that I greatly appreciated his offer, but that I had other business to attend to, and perhaps next time. I told him I would also convey his thanks to my father and back to Ann Arbor I went.

In the coming years I did a lot of work in and around Chicago. It was really just common sense on the part of my employers. Bringing in an outside hitter pretty much guaranteed that they wouldn't be recognized by any of the locals. I was fairly well known in the underground and only a couple of hours away so when they needed something done, and especially when they needed it done quickly, the problem could be solved for them in as little as 24 hours. I did work in Detroit as well but I really preferred Chicago for a number of reasons, not the least of which was its ample supply of excellent Italian restaurants. The guys in Detroit pretty much used locals or guys from Cleveland and Philly on occasion, which suited me just fine. They call it the motor city but for me it was kind of a dump and I just preferred working elsewhere if I had the option. I would stop in to Soul Queen now almost every time I visited and I got to know Sid really well. I tried to stop in after the lunch rush so he could sit down and talk for a while. We would talk for hours about food, cooking, football, and some of the whacked out shit that he we had both seen growing up in our respective cities. Chicago had a ton of drive-bys which was something that just didn't happen in Italy. If we were going to shoot someone we wanted to be up close and personal. This, combined with a lack of automobiles made it impractical as well. Sid saw his first killing at eight years old and from then on knew to always keep his eyes open and his head down when walking the streets. He was married to a Mexican girl and they had two beautiful kids but after a while his wife began to become more like her mother and less like the girl Sid had married. Divorce was not far off and neither was big trouble for my friend.

———————————

Thirteen

One day in early November I was called for a meeting about a particularly sensitive job. The situation was one that nobody from the top down wanted to be involved in and I was soon to find out why. The contract they wanted me to accept was on a dirty cop from New Jersey. A scum bag was a scum bag, even if he was a cop. Unfortunately, killing an officer of the law still carried some heavy weight with it no matter what the reason. I could give two shits about the job itself, it was the after effects that concerned me. Cops had lots of cop friends and cop support and anyone who killed one of their brethren would have a bull's eye on his back until he himself was eventually killed or captured. The job paid 50 large, which was significantly higher than even the most difficult assignment, but the kicker was it couldn't look like a hit, and that complicated things. I was given some recent photos and a home address, and after looking everything over agreed to take the assignment. I really never had much of a choice and I knew it. If I had said no to a job so sensitive there was a very good chance I myself would have been whacked, so in that respect it made my decision a little easier. I immediately began making both mental and physical preparations for the task at hand. First, I went on a crash diet of apples, tomato juice, and vitamin supplements. I had learned this technique from a job years ago and if you needed to lose weight fast this was the ticket. It absolutely sucked as I was used to enjoying food and had a 250 pound frame to prove it. I wanted to drop 20 pounds minimum to alter my physical appearance and after two and a half weeks I had reached my goal. Once again the reason for an outside contractor was to eliminate the possibly of someone recognizing or remembering my face, and I took it very seriously. Next, I went out and purchased colored contacts, and had been letting my hair grow out, as opposed to my bi-weekly trim. I also grew a small goatee and began going to a tanning salon to further darken my light olive Sicilian skin. Last, I had my hair color altered from its usual black to a light sandy brown. I bought a completely new wardrobe which included a pair of shoes with a small shard of metal placed in the inside heal area of the left shoe. What this would accomplish was to produce an automatic and very visible limp that was easily observed by anyone I happened to encounter during the job. Again this was something I wasn't looking forward to having to endure but this was a very sensitive situation and every detail needed to be taken into account. You might think that this would make people take notice of you, when in fact the truth was quite the opposite. Just like anyone with a handicap, either physical or mental, people tended to overt their eyes and their attention after the initial glance, as if they thought that they might catch whatever it was you had. A lot of thinking and psychology goes along with this type of work and over the years I had become very familiar with the subtle nuances that often made the difference between being successful, or getting caught. I would dispose of all of my stuff after the job and as I packed my luggage with the new clothes and some surveillance equipment I had also bought, I made a mental checklist in my mind of anything that I might have forgotten. The next morning with my plane ticket in hand, along with a complete set of fake credentials and credit cards, I was off to the airport.

I was given two months to do the removal so at least I had a little time to think and plan. The first thing I did was to start watching the target, both at work and at home. Everybody has routines, even cops, and I quickly started to get a feel for the situation. Day time varied a little with me following the guy around watching him from a distance doing cop stuff, but night was when I was really starting to learn about him. This guy was a drinker and a chick hound with various sexual escapades and female partners. This was sure to make things a little easier, I just hadn't figured out the angle yet. On the weekends the cop's wife stayed at home and watched the kids as her husband went off to shake down dealers and take advantage of the local hook- ers, johns ,and underground card games that supplemented his income. Just when I was getting bored watching the wife in the yard, an idea came to me. The wife, I had noticed, had one night of fun during the week where she went to the local bowling alley with her girlfriends. The hubby stayed home and watched sports on television and the kids as she enjoyed a few brief hours of freedom. I had followed her once and took notice of the fact that she always did two things, dress up and let loose. I figured that she was pretty much ignored on the home front and on the next bowling night I confirmed my suspicions. She was waiting at the bar for another gin and tonic when I smiled at her and complimented her on her appearance. It was easy to be sincere as she was decent looking and although she acted a little coy at first I could tell she was eating it up. On her next trip up she simply smiled. I had learned not to be too pushy or obvious and it paid off on her third, and much quicker return trip to the bar. She asked me my name and told me hers as I quickly got her to relax with some light conversation about nothing. She asked me what I did and I lied and told her that I was a detective that had been tasked to an investigation in the area. She said what a coincidence, my husband is a cop too. That is a coincidence I agreed as we clinked our glasses together and both laughed. I gave her enough details to get her curiosity going but then changed the subject. She asked me if I was going to be in the area for long and I said only until my work was done. I then thanked her for the conversation and excused myself for the night.

The next week I showed up again at the bowling alley and she quickly found me seated at the bar drinking my drink. We took up the conversation where it had left off and she asked me how my case was going. I said it was going alright and that I had finally gotten some good pictures of the subject and his girlfriend engaged in some pretty compromising positions and that I felt that we were close to wrapping it up, or at least my part of it. She giggled and said she would love to see the photos as I knew she would, and after a little more girlish prodding on her part I laughed and said alright, but obviously you cannot tell a soul. She agreed, and when I opened the folder and started fanning through the various shots her mouth dropped and she was speechless. I pretended not to notice and made some wise ass remarks about what was going to happen when the guy's wife found out. She was standing there still speechless when I turned to her and asked if she was alright. She gathered herself for a moment and said she wasn't feeling well, and quickly walked out of the bowling alley. I figured that after seeing pictures of her husband banging some other broads she would be furious, and I jumped in my car to head over and listen for the fireworks to begin when she got home.

I had found a vacant house in the neighborhood earlier that was for sale and it gave me an excellent view of their place. I quietly pulled in to the unoccupied driveway and after a few minutes I watched as her grey minivan roared up to the house. She got out and slammed the door and as she walked up the sidewalk I could just imagine how this was going to play out. I hadn't yet decided on how I was going to kill the guy but I figured that a few nude photos would liven things up and at least provide some entertainment value for me in the mean time. I could hear the wife screaming at the husband and the husband screaming back denying everything and calling her a paranoid and delusional bitch. I had expected all of this and was chuckling to myself when I heard a break in the yelling of about two minutes, followed by three gun shots.

At our meeting a couple days later the first thing they asked me was how in the fuck did you get her to clip her own husband? I mean for Christ sake, she's gonna do at least a dime for offing her old man, if not longer. Even if she tries to claim some I'm a whack job, abused wife bullshit, she'll go down for ten years for killin' a cop. I smiled, just glad the job was done, and nodded my head quietly saying I know, all I can say is that sometimes things take a strange turn of events. After collecting my fee I figured that with another week left on my return ticket I might as well enjoy myself and I caught the subway over to Manhattan. I had never been to New York and had always wanted to so I found a very nice but unobtrusive hotel on the upper East side visiting a local salon to have my hair fixed and my facial hair removed and then went back to my room to enjoy a one and a half hour massage from a local girl that the concierge had highly recommended.

Her name was Isis and she was originally from Greece, so we hit it off quickly and I remember thinking to myself that I bet Diamo would like her too. She gave an amazing massage and when she finished I asked her about any really good restaurants in the area. She smiled and said silly you're in Manhattan. There's nothing BUT good restaurants. If they're not they go out of business much quicker than they went in to it. I said no, I want to eat at a place where you would eat and she rattled off a short mix of Greek, Italian, and even one Russian joint that she was very fond of. I asked her to join me for dinner and at first she refused, but once I assured her that I was looking for dinner company and not a blowjob, her face turned red, but she smiled, and she accepted.

I was curious about the Russian place. Diamo and I were half Russian from our biological father but neither of us had ever even had so much as a bowl of Borsch. As we entered I was in awe of the gorgeous interior from the beginning. The booths were all made of hand carved black oak and the seats were upholstered in Russian yak leather of white, grey, and deep burgundy. Being both in the restaurant business and a regular patron of many, I was always very curios and impressed with what other owners had done with their places. The waitress showed up with a bottle of some really good soviet made vodka that was resting in a wine cooler carved from a block of ice and waiting for our pleasure on a small stand placed next to our table that itself was made of hand carved red cherry, with a silver marble top. We talked for a while, letting the cold liquor warm our insides and she told me about her homeland. I sat back enjoying her accent and her smile more and more. After a while, it felt like a minute and it seemed like a day, the waitress appeared to guide us through our food selections. She explained the day's selections as well as items that were small plate tastings of some of the most incredible recipes I had ever heard. We laughed and chatted as our first course arrived, and then another, and another, and we had another bottle of vodka brought. At the end we went back to her studio apartment and nature took its place as we made love until the sun came shining in the next day. We slept for a few hours and awoke with the same hunger as from the night before. After we showered she took me to a neighborhood Jewish place for a wonderful breakfast of both entertainment and food. The place was just electric for so early in the day, and the people were engaged in a playful and familiar banter between those that were serving the morning meal, and those who were receiving it. It was amazing. We had a few more days together and then I had to go home, at least for a little while.

———————————————

Fourteen

I had a friend in Nashville, some time to kill, and a hunger for southern cooking, so I came to find myself sitting in the Detroit airport waiting for a connecting flight to Tennessee. I also had two pounds of purple haze high grade marijuana in my suitcase, along with a couple of fifths of my favorite bourbon, BJ Holiday-Private Keep and a couple grand in cash stashed snuggly in my carry on. This was way before intensive airport security or a greater degree of common sense on my part. Call it crazy, but I made this trip every few months with the same cargo in tow and never had a problem. As I sat looking across the aisle I noticed a biker looking dude, probably in his late fifties, with tattoos peeking out from the wrist area of his yellow windbreaker. Our eyes met, he smiled slightly, and I said you've got a couple of tats eh. He laughed and said Yeah, just a few. I'd always appreciated good tattoo work and asked if I could see them. I was bored, it was Detroit, what can I say, I wasn't really concerned with offending anyone, including my new acquaintance. Dude was cool and said sure, as he took off his jacket. Underneath he had a full body cover of art work along with a t-shirt that said Marion

Federal Penitentiary- Body Art Competition. Some of it was just jail house crap but much of it was actually really well done and as I stepped closer to observe he began to explain a slight history of his map. I said that he'd obviously done some time, and he agreed. I asked when he had gotten out, and he looked me right in the eye and said "what time is it."

This caused me to pause briefly, and after looking at my watch it was revealed that Sonny had been out of federal prison for all of about 45 minutes, after having done 12 years of a 15-year sentence. I asked him what he had done and he laughed and said boy you're pretty direct aren't you. I agreed that I was, not really giving it much though, and he asked me how old I was. I replied 26 and he said well let's just say that when I was your age I used to like to rob banks. You any good at it, I asked. Well I thought I was, that is until the feds came knocking on my door. I thought for a second, assumed that being from the south he was probably a bourbon fan and asked if he liked whiskey. He said what do you think and I figured he did so I asked if I could offer him his first drink as a free man. He smiled again and said a little early isn't it. I said suit yourself, but if I'm gonna hear some stories, which I figure I'm about too, I'm pouring a drink. He chuckled and said sure, I'll join you. I grabbed a couple plastic glasses with ice from the airport bar and poured us both a few fingers of the best bourbon I have ever had to this day, with no branch water needed. He began to tell me about some of his jobs and the crazy shit that went along with it. I had done plenty of crazy shit myself, but never robbed a bank, so I was thoroughly entertained and beginning to catch one hell of a buzz. We boarded the plane, drinks in hand, and proceeded to kill the rest of the fifth en-route to Nashville. When the plane touched down Sonny and I were both pretty ripped and it wasn't quite noon. My buddy Jake was waiting at the gate and gave me a quick bro hug as I introduced my new amigo. I asked if we could give him a lift anywhere and he said bullshit, let's party. You drank a whole fifth of your stash with me now let me pay you back. He had a couple grand from money he had earned in the joint and was itching to have some fun so I thought what the fuck, let's do it. We headed off to a local liquor store loading up on whiskey, vodka, tequila, and beer, all of which Sonny insisted on paying for and then on to a local strip joint that Jake was fond of. In the south strip joints have memberships. You pay a nominal membership fee, and can then bring in your own bottle. You just pay for the mix, that is if you use any. Jake was friends with the manager and had three ounces of pink Bolivian cocaine in his jacket so things got really wild, really fast. Pretty soon he was cutting lines right on the table sharing with the strippers and the manager, all in plain few, crazy like I said. We were doing so much blow that the whiskey was no longer having much impact and as it became dark outside we decided we wanted to mix it up and visit another bar. We tipped the girls with wads of cash and headed out. Just before jumping in my buddies souped up Mustang some bouncer, that didn't party and who we didn't know, came up with some skank complaining that we had stolen her panties. We all laughed and said we hadn't but she was starting to yell, the bouncer was starting to act like a bad ass, and our mood was starting to change. Carrying as much as we were carrying none of us wanted to deal with cops but this big farm boy bouncer was starting to get under our skin just the same. I was apparently the most sober and the self appointed voice of reason. Jake and Sonny wanted to stomp his ass and it was getting really close to the point of no return and bouncer boy had absolutely no idea what was about to come at him. Looking back I really thought he was just showing off hoping to get some tail later on for his chivalrous actions. What he did not realize was that if he didn't shut up and back off, and I mean now, the only place he was going to end up was the local E.R. or worse. Finally, I got him where only he and I could be heard, looked up straight into his eyes (he was a big boy) and said dude, I'm sure you don't make shit working here and I guarantee you don't have medical insurance as a bouncer. You are about to get fucked up really bad. I don't want that and neither do you, so walk away, take the bitch with you, make an excuse, fuck her later, I don't really care, but leave us alone. This is the last time I'm going to tell you. I don't know you, and I don't owe you jack shit, but quite frankly I don't feel like dealing with any of what I know is about to happen, and you don't, so split, okay. He must have had a guardian angel, an ounce of common sense, or a little of both, but off he went, with the skank still running her mouth. As we got into the car and drove off we all started to decompress and laugh about what just happened. We all agreed that old boy had balls that was for sure, just as the pair of panties came slingshoting into the front seat from the back seat, with Sonny laughing hysterically. Son of a bitch...

I thought we were going to wind down but Sonny had other plans and a new found alliance in my buddy Jake and said hey, I know of a really nice local whore house, my treat. I said that I wasn't up for catching the clap right now and he said that it was a clean house, honest. He had just gotten out of the joint and how the hell he knew anything about a local place was beyond me but Jake had a taste for strange apparently, so off we went. The establishment was in a part of Nashville called the nations, a place where there were two things you did not find; cops or white boys. Great I thought. I wasn't carrying a gun, and tough as we might have been we would be no match for a gang of ghetto brothers if they decided to jump us. As we pulled into the driveway of the large house I noticed how, unlike all of the run down shacks that surrounded it, this place was actually pretty well maintained. It had a huge back yard with plenty of bushes, trees, and flowers, with a nice veranda off the back porch. It was like some place out of Gone with the Wind in only in the ghetto. We walked up on the front porch, ringing the bell, as a booming voice from inside said come in! As we walked into the front foyer a very large black dude of about 50 was sitting upright on a hospital bed just to the left of us, a sawed off 12- gauge on his lap, a glass of Courvoisier and coke within arm's reach, along with several bottles of pain killers on the night stand. Sonny, when did you get out the joint brother!! Sonny jumped over to him, giving him a big hug, and said excitedly, just this morning my brother! Lewis was the purveyor of this fine brothel, and as brief introductions were made he said what you boys got a taste for? Sonny was the first to reply, laid down a$1,000 and said brother I've been showering with dudes for so long I want to try everything on the menu. They both laughed out loud and Lewis said well alright then. He pushed a buzzer on the side of the bed and the parlor door opened as a very lovely Asian African sister motioned us to come in. For the next two days we were treated like kings and I know we got way more than a $1,000 worth, but no one said anything and we damn sure didn't complain. There were 14 girls in the house and Lewis's wife was one of the best soul food cooks I had ever enjoyed. Half way through the first night she came out of the kitchen to offer us a cup of tea and I thought sure, why not. What I didn't know was that it was mushroom tea and would start us on a very interesting 48 hour journey. We ate, enjoyed the ladies, slept, watched movies, and did it all again, over and over for two days straight. I had that purple haze and first I asked Lewis if it was cool. He said sure, long as you share. I gave him an ounce of it for his personal use and proceeded to roll a bunch of joints for the rest of us. Later one of the girls walked up and handed me a chunk of something wrapped in foil and said it was a gift from Lewis. I opened it up to reveal a glistening black chunk of pure opium, perfumy as hell and ripe for smoking. Our time just spiraled into one big time span but what a time it was...

I had little doubt the girls were actually pretty clean but I still wore rubbers and no one was offended. Honestly, I was having such a good time I didn't really care about much and I did not want to leave. I could tell that Sonny and Lewis were tight as brothers and had missed each other a great deal. When it came time to roll we thanked them all for their hospitality and Lewis said you all come back any time you hear. Lewis and Sonny hugged one more time and I could tell they were both a little sad from having to end the weekend. We dropped Sonny at the bus station and finally headed to Jake's house.

Jake had left to pick me up at the airport, and that had been three days ago. Man was his wife pissed when we walked in...

Fifteen

Sid and is wife had been on the rocks for a while know so when I got his phone call telling me they were getting a divorce I wasn't that surprised. The next thing his said however threw me back a few. Christiana, his wife, had a brother who was pretty high up in one of the local street gangs. He was her older brother and apparently had the whole Big Bro thing going on so when Christiana or C as everybody called her told her brother some bad and completely false shit about Sid the brother had put a mark on my friends head for ten grand. Sid was shitting a brick. He knew the brother, knew he was serious, and knew that he had the network and resources to see that the job was completed. This was a touchy situation for me. I loved Sid like a brother but this was not my town and it wasn't my problem, so I had to chew on it for a bit. After a while I came to my decision and realized that I could not allow my friends kids to become orphans, especially over some trumped up bullshit that wasn't even half true. I told him to stay away from the restaurant and his house until I got down there as this would be the first place I would pick to hit someone if it were me. I didn't know what timeline if any the brother had set but I wasn't going to wait and find out and was sitting with Sid at a local diner in uptown the next day. He told me how C was pissed at him after finding out he been dipping his wick with another girl. I said bro that was your first mistake as he went on. She had said he was beating her and the kids which anyone who knew the dude would see as impossible. He wasn't a drinker or a doper and had no temper what so ever. The thought of him smacking his old lady around, and especially his beloved children was simply unbelievable and I knew in my heart it was a malicious lie meant born out of malice, and nothing else.

My first question was if I could possibly just talk to the guy and figure things out on a professional level. Brother or not I knew if this guy had been on the streets for any measure of time at all he would know, as I did, that women were first and foremost attached to their feelings and not necessarily rational thought from birth forward. Sid told me that I would never even make it into the barrio where the gangs operated, much less arrange a conversation with someone as high up as this. I disagreed and there was no street in the world that I was afraid of walking down. He said first of all Dominick your white, and I thought Jesus Christ here we go again. He said no dude I don't have a problem with it but in that part of town you're going to stick out even more than you would here. The people watch the streets carefully and they know who belongs and who does not, and they handle their business very quickly. I needed to think about it and I needed to eat, so we headed over to Lincoln Park for one of my favorite mom and pop Italian joints called Topo Gigio. In Italian roughly translated it was the name of a cartoon character much like the American Mickey Mouse. I didn't know how they had come up with the name but the food was fantastic. They didn't do a lot of fancy shit the just cooked from scratch and used good ingredients. Everything from the first slice of bread to the last cannoli was flat out incredible and they had only 12 tables so it could get very busy very fast. We lucked out and got a table easily as it was early evening in the middle of the week. Midway through dinner Sid seemed to relax and I told him that we needed to get him to a hotel for a few days just to lay low, and I wasn't sure just how yet, but I was confident I could fix the problem one way or the other.

After we found a suitable hotel I got the address of the brother and went out to do some initial scouting of the area. Once again I had a rental car as I always did and this time I had opted for a brand new charcoal colored Lincoln MKX. I wasn't looking to stand out but one thing I knew about the streets was that a nice ride, driven with the right attitude, could allow you to enter places a piece of shit beater simply could not. I had picked a car with dark limo tint and being that it was already dark assumed that I would not stand out to much. I was right and as I cruised the area I began to formulate a possible plan. Sid had told me that the brother was married, but like many people with authority had a girlfriend on the side. Americans saw this much differently than the majority of the rest of the world. In every country from Asia to Zimbabwe guys who had power got laid, it was that simple. If you were a boss in the corporate world or on the streets, women were attracted to you. I don't know if it was the thrill of it, the danger, which all women admit it or not are drawn to or just being able to fuck a guy who could afford to show them a good time, but bosses had their choice of female company. Always have and always will. I went back to the hotel and spent the next few hours drawing a sketch of the barrio from memory, making notes, and writing out any questions or variables I was concerned with. It had been a long day and after a 20 minute shower I fell into a deep sleep. When I woke up the next day I made a phone call to a friend of mine who could get hard to find items. Sid and I then headed out to get some breakfast and enjoy the city a little bit. I knew that my best hours of operating for this job would be after dark so I filled the days with my brother from another mother and having a little fun. Sid was pretty nervous but I assured him that soon enough he would be back home and back cooking at the Soul Queen. This seemed to calm him down, if only for a few hours and for now that was good enough. The package I had requested arrived and I began to put my plan into gear.

Dilaudid is normally prescribed for severe pain at an average dosage of 2 to 4 mg four times daily. I had a 100 mg bottle in liquid from shipped to me at a local post office box along with syringes, IV needles and drip bag. I found a pay by the month storage unit a few miles from the target and paid cash for three months up front. Next, I visited a local junker car lot and purchased an older model sedan with a fast engine just in case. I had darkened my skin with liquid tan and purchased some clothes more suited to the barrio I would be now walking through to do my close up reconnaissance. After a couple of more days I had figured out the brother basic habits and patterns and I got ready to put my plan to work. He stayed home at night three nights a week and usually in the middle of it. On Thursday or Friday however, he always went out to a local night club with his girlfriend and they always ended up back at her apartment, which lucky for me was in a really quiet neighborhood a good distance from the barrio. From a distance she looked to be some Caucasian broad that probably worked in an office and I just figured the dude had a taste for mashed potatoes and white bread on occasion. As they say variety is the spice of life and I just thought fuck it, this just makes my job that much easier and I smiled to myself as I got ready to take him.

I had made a small spray bottle of 20 mgs of the drug combined with alcohol and olive oil and as I watched them pull up to her apartment after their usual night of partying I waited for the apartment lights to go off. I popped the lock on his car with relative ease and disabled the factory alarm quickly. Wearing disposable latex gloves I sprayed the leather steering wheel, locked it back up and went to wait in my car for him to come out. I had parked on the same side of the street so that I would be able to pull out and follow him closely without causing much suspicion. It was early spring and I knew that he would have no reason to wear gloves and as he came out I noticed a grin on his sexually satisfied face, a confident bounce to his step, and unprotected hands. He fired his car up along with a cigarette and turned on some music as he pulled out. I followed at a slight distance, clearly able to observe his silhouette through the rear window of his car. After a few minutes I noticed him start to swerve a little and I could see his head and neck begin to get more and more relaxed. It was three am and we were still in a quiet neighborhood, so at the next stop sign I bumped his car from behind with mine and he stopped just as planned. I quickly got to his driver's side and as he rolled down the window I could tell the drugs had done their job, soaking into his bare skin from the saturated steering wheel of the car. He looked at me and said what the fuck in Spanish as I told him it was all good and shot him up with another dose of dope. I easily pushed his now limp body over to the passenger's side and drove off leaving my junker still running and parked in the middle of the road.

When he came to I had him comfortably strapped into a steel chair that I had previously mounted to the cement floor of the storage unit. I had already taped him up with an IV in case I actually needed plan B. I didn't think I would but as my mother used to say it's always good to have a plan B, so I had one. He started to get mad calling me all kinds of bad names in his native tongue and saying that whatever rival gang I represented me and my whole crew would feel the reprisal of his gang whether I killed him or not. Some of this was real, but some of it was bravado, and I knew the difference. I spoke to him with respect and this was simply to lay the foundation for a solution that didn't end in me taking his life. I explained the situation to him as I understood it and first assured him that, love his sister or not, she had lied. What this did was to allow him an out from feeling that he had to defend her. Saving face is a huge and valuable tool in any kind of negotiating unfortunately, many people were just to apathetic or too fucking dumb to utilize it to their benefit. I explained to him that neither I nor Sid had any desire to have this problem go any further and were willing to pay him to make it go away. The one thing I made very clear to him however, without being cocky in the least, was to explain that I had gotten to him and I could do it again with relative ease. I further explained that this was really the last thing I felt like wasting my time doing and would greatly prefer that we come to an agreement. I don't know if it was because he knew I could kill him or if like me he had much bigger fish to fry than an ex brother-in-law, but we were able to come to an understanding. I offered him the extra twenty grand I had kept from the pawn shop loot, and after a little hesitation on his part even offered up the additional ten grand in gold jewelry I had kept, but told him not to get greedy as this was my final offer.

I wanted him happy but I didn't want him that happy and I sure as hell didn't need to open the goddamn door for a shakedown after I left town.

I assured him that this matter would remain between he and I and I suggested he tell C that Sid had simply paid him off to remove the contract. It was believable and partially true. It would allow him to retain his image both with his sister and with his crew and this was really the main thing that mattered after all, and I knew it.

Sixteen

Diamo had graduated and moved out to Seattle a few years ago to take an internship at a local hospital. This would eventually lead to him becoming one of the most respected heart surgeons in the western United States. Our parents and I were very proud of him and Papa insisted on flying us all out to Sicily for a graduation party and family reunion. I had been dating Isis for a while now and she joined me on the flight across the Atlantic to visit my homeland. When we got there it was much as I had remembered with some subtle differences. There were many more cars although horses were still very much in use. The customs had not changed however and my mother and father both showered us with hugs and kisses, and then turned their affection to Isis and Diamo's wife and two children. Bambino!! mother exclaimed for this was the first time she had met her grandkids. It was incredible to see her this happy again and she spent every waking moment of the next ten days cooking and singing, playing games with the children and asking all of us about our time in America. It was very much like when Angelia was still alive and as I sat back to just watch, my brother came up with a glass of

Grappa and sat beside me to catch up on our own lives. I was so happy to see our parents dancing with joy that this in itself would have been enough but lately I hadn't seen my brother very often so it was really the best of both worlds. Diamo began telling me about his life, his career, and his beautiful family. Since leaving Ann Arbor he had worked his ass off as I knew he would and was now living a very busy and quite comfortable existence. He asked me about my life and I told him about Hero's and some of the investments I had made along the way which had proved to be very fruitful. We both acknowledged that we had enjoyed a very good teacher in our father, as we drained our glasses and refilled them again. He didn't ask about the other stuff and I didn't volunteer. He had heard some stories that made the newspapers on occasion, but nothing with my name in it so I just let it rest. He said that sometimes he missed the hustle and the action that we had as children here in Sicily and I laughed as I said that while it certainly had its moments, it also had its draw backs, much like anything else. We spent the rest of our days just enjoying our time with the people we loved and gorging ourselves on mothers abundant home cooking.

I told Diamo how a big pharmacy and convenience chain had been trying to buy the building that I had Hero's in. I had purchased it years ago as the landlord wanted to retire and even with the princely sum I had originally paid for it, I would still make almost a million dollars off the impending sale of the building.

I had also decided that even though I would no longer need the income I had a great staff who all loved and needed their jobs. When I did actually sell the following year I bought another building four blocks away, that while needing some structural improvements was still a great investment at a great price. We moved Hero's, expanding both the dining room and our catering operations, and still had room to divide off and rent to three other tenants, who when combined paid much more than the monthly note on the property. I was once again very fortunate and eventually decided to sell the sub shop end of the business to my three long time staff who had always been both great at their jobs and had always demonstrated an unquestionable loyalty to both me and the business. Our only other competition was a local main stay called Zimmerman's Deli which was nothing like what we did, but had an absolutely amazing menu and was growing every year. I actually ate there at least once a week and one time, while enjoying a huge pastrami sandwich with homemade pickle a Hero's customer approached me to ask why on earth I would be eating here when I made such good subs. I could only reply that first, like everyone else I occasionally got sick of subs and this was sort of the same logic behind why I would never choose to be a gynecologist. Secondly, I said, in this town there's plenty of business for everyone and I am not a greedy man. They smiled as if they understood but their eyes clearly showed that they did not. I didn't really care either way, and went back to my lunch.

Diamo asked me how I had survived this long in the business we both knew about, but did not speak of. I said that a big part of it was very simple; trust but verify. Every one, every time...

Father drove us around the city and surrounding countryside in his shiny new Cadillac SUV that he had shipped over from the States. Diamo and I had offered to pay for it when he had first announced ordering one in the previous year and even over the phone from a thousand miles away I could hear the pride in his voice as he politely declined our offer. After a few days he had asked me if I wanted to visit Angelia's grave at our family cemetery. I had been thinking about it and had even confided in Isis my thoughts. I had hoped that she would not feel slighted and she explained that she was not in the least bit. She further explained that although she now loved me with all of her heart, she also knew, as is the case with every one of us, that she was not my first love, nor I hers. I was so happy that she understood and the next day father, Diamo, and I drove out to visit Angelia's grave. We had brought a large bouquet of fresh flowers and upon arrival noticed that the grave as well as those around it had all been neatly maintained. Angelia's plot had flowers that appeared perhaps a week old and as father bent down to replace them he told us that the cemetery had become one of his projects to stay active. That was so typical of him. He could have easily paid someone to do the work but this was family and it was personal. So as a man well into his 70s he had made the trip every week. He had a small shed built on the property with a lawn mower and a few tools to perform his tasks without having to load his car for every trip. I noticed a wooden bench with a sturdy back and a very nice padded seat placed on the knoll overlooking her grave and he explained that on occasion mother would join him. As he went about his work she would sit on the bench and quietly knit or crochet as she gazed out over the calm blue water. He said that although they both missed Angelia since her passing and both of us since our departure. They also knew that life was full of change and if you wanted to survive you must eventually accept it and move on. We could not have asked for two better people to call parents and while in my line of work I no longer communicated very often with a higher being, I took the time in that moment to thank God for both of them.

As our vacation came to an end we were all very sad for we realized that our visits in the future would be very few, if at all. Father and mother were growing older, Diamo had a busy life with his practice and his family, and Iris and I were talking about having kids of our own. I knew that coming back to Sicily was just a matter of taking the time and planning it. We all had suffi-cient money to do it unfortunately, time was increasingly becom-ing in short supply. We all agreed to try and we left it at that. Mother and father had bought small gifts for each of us to take home including two small stuffed animals they hoped Iris and I would give to our babies in the near future. Mother gave us all a hug that I was sure would break her arms she kissed all of the babies, and then excused herself as father grabbed his car keys to take us to the airport. We were all leaving again and I knew although we wished it wouldn't. It hurt our mother very much.

Seventeen

True to his word Mr. Wolfe had become tired of Ireland. Since the McCabe family went down the local magistrate had enjoyed an increasing efficiency at prosecuting street crime, and he knew his days were numbered. The Wolfe had been roughing people up since he was just a boy, and had killed almost as many so with the law of averages it was just a matter of time before they caught up to him. He had bought a place in Spain that wasn't very big but overlooked the Mediterranean with an average daily temperature much more to his liking that the one in Limerick. He had visited a few times already, making a few friends and entertaining the affections of a local Señora. He would have to get used to the food and the beer, or lack thereof, but it was a small consideration for what was about to come.

One day there came a knock at the door as he thought it might. The local constables quickly advised him of the circumstances for his arrest and placed him with two pairs of hand irons behind his back. Normally they only required one but do to the Wolfe's large frame and gigantic arms they knew they could never properly transport him with just a single pair. At least they were considerate enough to do that. The police had been well aware of his activities for many years, and while it had taken until recently to acquire enough solid evidence to convict, when it came time for the trial they had more than enough to put him away for life. He had limited visits from a few people, Sean included, as he awaited sentencing in the stark Irish jail house. He'd been warned not to go as he too was on the short list but Mr. Wolfe wasn't just a friend, and Sean figured the Garda could all just piss off. They spoke about things, both in the past and those to come, and unbeknown to anyone listening, they made a plan to get him out. They both knew that once sentence had been passed he would have a snowballs chance in hell of ever seeing the rolling hills of Ireland as a free man ever again. Irish prisons where notoriously hard and many blokes never lived past the first 30 from either another man's shank, disease, or the beating that most took as an introduction to the yard. Wolfe had enemies both on the street and in the joint so options were few and he knew he had to take a chance.

The courthouse stood on the banks of a river and the holding cells along with a small infirmary sat in the rear of the building overlooking the cold black water. Just before his time to be brought into the court room he faked chest pain and collapsed on the ground. While the guards thought he might just be carrying on they didn't want to lose their jobs over a prisoner dying and they helped him to rest on a white gurney in the corner of the room. He acted like he was barely conscious and with a man of his size the guards became much more relaxed than they should have. They unlocked the cuffs and where preparing to secure his ham sized hands to the rails of the medical bed when his eyes got wide and he let loose with a punch that dropped the bigger of the two guard's stone cold on the floor. He leapt off the gurney and easily over powered the other guard as he growled give me your fucking keys. The windows had security barriers and locks, but the guards all had keys and after putting the other fellow to rest the Wolfe unlocked the steel gate and jumped into the frigid November water below. Watching from a short distance Sean quickly ferried the small motor boat across to rescue his wet and freezing friend and they sped off into the distance 20 minutes before anyone in the courthouse was the wiser. The soaking man quickly changed into the wool sweater and jeans on the boat and as he greedily sipped hot tea and Jameson's from a thermos on board, thanked his friend for the act of bravery. Sean kept his eye on the water and said no thanks needed. You'd have done the same for me and I know it.

Ireland was immediately too hot for the escaped convict to remain in and as he shoved off that night for his new home he took Sean's hand in his own and said brother if your ever in Spain, and he began to choke on his words. Like Sean, the Wolfe had never enjoyed many true friends and having to leave one behind took him pretty hard. I know, I know, and Sean gave his large associate a strong hug as he said now off with you before the Garda catches you again and puts your great big Irish ass back in the box for good...

The boat crossed the English Channel with the Wolfe puking at random over the starboard side. He never had been much on boats or planes for that matter, but beggars aren't the choosers and he shut up as he enjoyed the ride to freedom. They docked on the western side of Spain and with a car waiting easily made their way over the next day to the eastern side of the island and Valencia where he had bought his villa. Spain did not have an extradition agreement with Ireland but still he kept a low profile at first. He bought a small pub that was somewhat popular with the tourists but didn't make much profit, and truth be told the Wolfe still had a flavor for his old life. One of the main businesses was imported hashish that was shipped over from countries across the sea, repackaged, and trucked north to the other European countries. While he had never had much involvement in the drug trade the rules were pretty much the same and the money was even better. He started out just running security for a few shipments. Just as the drug runners where always trying to make money the other criminals were always trying to take it from them. On his second trip north they were driving along in the early hours of the morning with the young driver complaining that he always had a hard time staying awake with these midnight runs. The Wolfe suggested a cup of coffee or perhaps turning on the radio as this always worked for him. The driver kept on and said no, it's just something I'll never get used to either way. If it wasn't for the money I would tell the boss to go screw himself and be back at home sleeping in my own bed right now. A few kilometers further along they were suddenly stopped by a large truck blocking their path and a man with a shotgun approached, shining a light in their faces as he got closer. The Wolfe got out with his hands up and asked what do we have here then. The Frenchman with the gun and an accent replied that what we have is a hijacking my friend. Now keep your hands up while we unload your goods and you'll be on your way just as safe as a new born baby. The Wolfe smiled as the slightly unaware man began to walk past him and reaching into the hidden pocket inside the collar of his overcoat he grasped the ball hammer that he always kept. In an instant he brought the lethal object down onto the Frenchman's skull with a loud crunch. Dead before he hit the ground and slightly hidden because of the darkness, the Wolfe picked up the shotgun, turned and pumped one round directly into the chest of the hijacker's approaching partner. He quickly ran to the other truck and before the driver could start the motor, blew his head partially off his shoulders with another round of twelve gauge buckshot. He pulled the dead driver out and discarded him in the ditch. Starting the truck he pulled it over onto the side of the road, threw the keys into the bushes, and walked back to do the same with the other bodies. When he got back to his own truck his two associates just looked at him with a mixture of fear and uncertainty. He slid into the cab, lit up a Dunhill, inhaled deeply, and said with a laugh well I guess that will wake you up then.

He established himself in Spain just as easily as he had in his homeland and within a matter of months the pub was simply a place he enjoyed and never again relied on for income. The weather was much easier on his bones and he made love to the Spanish señora every night after yet another wonderful meal from the nearby sea. She was as fine a cook as she was a lover and would make them sumptuous paellas from rice, shrimp or langoustines', clams, mussels, and octopus, with a combination of roasted peppers and onions in a spicy tomato broth. He remembered Sean talking about how they ate in Sicily and he smiled as he thought of his friend sitting beside him drinking a glass of the Spanish red wine and enjoying one of his girlfriend's meals. Many nights she and he had gone into town to have tapas at one of the local bodegas. Spain was well known for ham and olives as well as several excellent goat or sheep's milk cheese varieties. It was much different than what he was used to but he quickly acquired both a taste and appreciation for all that his new country had to offer. The one thing that hadn't changed however, was his opinion of a snitch and this was soon to be tested once more.

Spain had a significant percentage of Basque people in its population. Like the Celts that Wolfe was born of the Basques were fiercely independent, distrusting of the government, and had both a passion for living and a temper that were unequalled in other cultures. The biggest single attribute of any Basque person was trust and to violate it was a guarantee of either excommunication or death. Late on Friday night one of his partners came by to inform that the police had gotten one of their shipments to Germany. It never made it out of the country and while they both knew that occasionally the police would get lucky, in Spain they had made enough payoffs to insure that they didn't happen on this side of the fence. The next day after a few inquiries were made they found out that one of their mid-level associates had gotten picked up the last month for a bullshit street deal. This in itself wasn't that unusual. What was strange however was how easily he walked. The man in question had enough strikes that he should have at minimum done two years and he didn't even do two nights. The Wolfe had some of his guys track him down and instructed them to bring him up to the hotel where he kept an office on the fourth floor. As they dragged the now trembling man into the room it wasn't too far off to consider that they had their rat. The Wolfe offered him a smoke and suggested that he make it easy on every one and just come out with it. Even with sweat breaking on his brow the man began to profess his innocence, which everyone in the room thought was ironic and stupid, as no one had even said what they suspected him of. It could have been just skimming which, while still getting him a hospital stay, would not have warranted a killing. Pretty soon the Wolfe became both angry and insulted. He had been looking forward to a night on the town with his lovely and now this lying, rat motherfucker, was not only keeping him from enjoying himself, he was pissing on his floor to top it off. Strip him, handcuff him the Wolfe said and put him in the janitors closet. The man knew what this meant as he had witnessed firsthand his employers rage in the past. They had a man stealing from them the past year and when confronted he had denied everything, even though they already knew he was ripping them off. They stripped the man, handcuffed him, and put him on a chair with plastic underneath it. The Wolfe calmly approached, hammer in hand, and with a sickening crunch systematically took out first one kneecap, then the other. He paused to let the man vomit from the pain, and then resumed with a strike to one collar bone, then the other, with the elbows, toes, testicles, and finally the top of the head to follow. The man had died but he had died in incredible fucking pain and that is exactly what they had planned for him.

As he stood now completely naked in the closet he began to ponder his fate. The room had a small window, just big enough to climb through, but it was solid glass and he was both naked and on the fourth floor, with his hand secured behind him. He could hear the men talking and he knew it was just a matter of minutes before he would meet the same violent death as the thief. As the Wolfe poured a dram of whiskey they all heard a window shatter and ran to the closet to see what it was. The prisoner was gone and the window was completely broken out. As he stuck his head out the now empty frame he saw the naked man running off still very much alive. The man had decided that attempting to jump, even from 40 feet up was better than waiting to have your nuts and your kneecaps crushed, so out the window he dove. As luck would have it the rain from the previous night had softened the ground and while he dislocated his shoulder and broke two ribs in the fall, he was still able to escape, running down the street startling the passersby with his hands still in cuffs, and his cock and balls dangling out for everyone to see. The Wolfe just grinned and thought that at least now he could meet his girl and maybe have a go at the night after all.

A few days later the brother of the man showed up saying he had a package in the back of his old truck. Tied securely in the bed of the rusty vehicle and laying among old wine bottles and pig shit, was the informant now completely spent and covered in a dirty tarp. The Wolfe ordered him to bring the truck around to the rear loading dock, and when he did his men removed the pale figure from the vehicle. He reached into his jacket and pulled out a roll of cash which the brother declined. The Wolfe looked at him oddly and said you won't accept money? To which the man looked him straight on and said I cannot accept money for turning in my brother but I can't have a brother who's an informant either. He got in his truck, started the engine, and drove away without ever looking back.

———————————

Eighteen

East St Louis was much like other cities in America that had fallen victim in the past decade to gang activity and the rampant drug addiction that supported it. Doris Meeks had come from a good family but crack cocaine among other bad choices had lead to her calling an abandoned shack by the river home for herself and her 11 year old son Ben. She bounced between working the streets giving head jobs for twenty bucks, and shoplifting to support both her habit and the tiny amount of food she would get for the two of them. The abandoned house they lived in had a roof that didn't just leak but actually had water pouring in when the frequent rain storms came. They had made the laundry room in the back of the main floor their sleeping area as it seemed to stay the driest and also seemed the most secure as it had a door to the back yard that had been ply wooded over and was now permanently closed. Their minimal belongings consisted of only a few blankets, a worn out and filthy full sized mattress that they both shared, a camp stove that was falling apart but still worked for warming up soup cans and water for instant coffee, and a worn photo that Ben kept hidden that showed the life they used to live before his mom's drug addiction and subsequent divorce. He had wanted to stay with his dad and had pleaded with the court to let him. Unfortunately, his father, while a much better choice as a parent, had two drunk driving convictions on his record and the scum bag lawyer his mom was fucking in exchange for representation had used this to persuade the judge to give the young mother full custody. They had lived in a three bedroom ranch in the suburbs of St. Louis but his mom soon lost both the house and her job to her drug habit, and had fled with an outstanding warrant taking her son to a part of the city she assumed no one would ever find them in.

One of the local thugs, a dude that went by the street name of Big Time had been trying to get Doris to work for him on the block. He occasionally flipped her some free dope to wet her appetite but the most he ever got back was some nasty white ass that barely even made him pop a nut. He did however let the disheveled women come over to his crib on occasion to use the shower. One night while he was smoking a joint outside with his boys, Doris came upon his stash and, after and looking around for witnesses, she frantically stuffed it into her soiled panties. As she came out of the house she told him she had to get back to her son and he nodded his head and said cool mama, check you later. After she left it didn't take Big Time long to notice his shit gone and he knew without question where to find it. Doris and Ben were sleeping on the musty mattress in the back of the house when the crack dealer and his crew busted in. Ben tried to defend his mom and one of the posse busted him over the head with a short baseball bat. With her son laying in a filthy pile of trash and his own blood she began to search her burned out brain for plausible excuses, none of which Big Time was buying for a second. First, she simply denied it and he punched her directly in the face as she heard the crunch of her own nose shattering and felt the warm red liquid of life beginning to cover her chin and t-shirt. She said she would give it back, and he laughed out loud and said you damn right you gonna give it back. You gonna give something else too bitch!! She produced the drugs hoping that he would simply fuck her and leave them alone. Doris had no idea what these street thugs were capable of but she was soon to find out. There were four of them and while two of them held her down they spent the next two hours fucking her in every orifice, punching her in the face when they felt like it, and repeatedly lighting and then putting out blunts on various areas of her exposed flesh, breast, and vagina. When they had had their fill one of the punks said what about the kid as he pointed to the still unconscious young Ben on the floor. Fuck him, and fuck her, shoot them both, and without so much as a second thought he walked up and shot the young man in the head, turned and did the same to Doris.

A week later another homeless person found the two bodies and even in the advanced state of decomposition the local police soon surmised it had been a brutal death for both of the two victims. Fortunately, Doris had a state issued ID and within a day her family had been notified of the death of both their sister and her son. Captain Frank Staten was just getting home from work when his wife gave him the news. He hadn't been close to his sister in recent years but it was still his sister, and she had been brutally murdered in a rundown shit hole in a part of town she never should have even been in. Frank had been with the force for 20 years and had a younger brother who was a CO at the local jail, and they both new that even if the punks who did this were caught they could probably plea bargain it down to a short sentence of five to ten, and be out in three years with good behavior. As it turned out the shooter had gotten caught while driving a stolen car higher than a kite with the murder weapon still on him. When he came down he mistakenly thought the cops already knew about the murder and started talking and asking for a deal. They rounded up Big Time and the rest of them and they all tried to put the blame on one another in exchange for a reduced sentence. They may not have graduated high school, but they all knew exactly how the system worked. What they didn't know was that the victims were the family of a police officer and the prosecutor wasn't cutting any deals. At the trial the arrogant defendants all bragged openly about how they had done it and Big Time smirked as he looked at her family and described fucking that white junky bitch in the ass, and using her pussy for my own personal ashtray. They received the max of 20 to life and were scheduled to be transported to the maximum security prison up state as soon as four beds opened up. The corrections department said it would be about one month but the jail had plenty of space and they could stay put in the mean time. The brothers wanted them to pay for what they had done and neither could get out of their minds the laughing court room confessions or the cocky smiles that went along with it. They were at a loss for vengeance when Frank remembered talking to Doris's ex husband at the funerals. The husband was a soul brother who not only wanted revenge for his ex wife and son as bad as they did, but supposedly had some family members that were connected to the St Louis underworld. Frank was on the opposite side of the law from these types but he wanted his sister avenged so the next day he made a call to the ex.

With Doris' husband vouching for him a meeting was scheduled. At the meeting the local street boss, a black dude named Wesley, said first let me offer my condolences, and Frank knew he was sincere. He went on to explain that they had long been associated with people who could handle such matters but secrecy was a must for obvious reasons. Frank asked about costs and was told that while typically such a matter would be expensive to resolve, in this case he would cover the costs with one request. He explained that with both Frank and his brother's occupations they could offer an invaluable amount of support to the execution of the operation and Frank told him that as for him he would do whatever he could to help, but his brother would need to give his own word of acceptance to the terms. That night he spoke with his younger brother, and after a few beers and a few shots of Jameson they both agreed to offer their help, and I flew to St Louis the next week to meet with Wesley.

We knew they were being moved in the next few weeks and time was of the essence. I asked why we couldn't just put a contract on them once they reached the prison. It would be much easier and for $500 each they were already dead men from a shank to the kidney from any number of willing assassins in the prison yard. Wesley explained that normally that would have been an option, however the people they had killed and the way they had killed them warranted a very different method be used. This was a revenge hit and they had been distant family of his, so these animals were going to suffer. I started getting a plan together and within eight days we were ready to act. The first thing I did was to assess the route from the jail to the prison. The trip would take the jail transport approximately 120 miles north, with the four targets shackled securely in the rear of the vehicle with a cage dividing them from the two guards riding in the front seat. Once they left the city the majority of the ride would take them through countryside and farmland. I was able to find a house with a barn and 20 acres that sat 20 miles east of the midway point of the transport route, and had a closest neighbor of almost one half mile away. I ordered some supplies from the same friend I had used on the Sid's in-law job, and after a brief meeting with the two brothers we were ready to go with just 24 hours notice.

I got familiar with the house I had rented and the owners had explained that they would be vacationing at their winter home in Florida for the next several months so I knew I wouldn't be getting any company. I had used a cover as a research professor from a small college and asked them before they left if the area had any bee farmers that I could possibly interview for my research. They gave me the number of a man a half an hour away and after meeting him and observing his hives I persuaded him to sell me one active bee box for my research. He packaged my purchase in black plastic to keep the inhabitants calm during the drive back. I had purchased an old pickup truck for my work and he easily loaded the active, live bee hive into the back, and suggested I invest in a bee suit if I didn't want to get stung more than I already would be from my research. I thanked him for his time and advise promising to indeed buy a suit, as I returned to the farm to unload my buzzing friends. I hadn't gotten notice of an impending prisoner transport yet so I continued to make preparations on the farm. I went to a local rental company and arranged for an excavator to be delivered to the property and paid for two weeks rental before I left. They asked if I needed to hire an operator and I thanked them but said I was quite capable of operating the equipment by myself. I explained that it had been a few years however and wondered if they would mind spending a half an hour with me at the rental yard to refresh my memory prior to the delivery. It was actually kind of fun and with a little practice I felt confident that I could easily accomplish the task I had in mind. The next day they delivered the large piece of equipment and I went to work digging a hole approximately 12 feet deep and 10 feet wide, with a sloping ramp at one end that I could easily drive a prisoner transport van down into. I parked the excavator in the barn, went into the house to shower off, and then drove 20 minutes away to an excellent little mom and pop dinner for some much needed supper.

Two days later I got the call I had been waiting for and I headed back to St. Louis to make ready for the snatch. We got the transport scheduled for night time which wasn't all that unusual. With the help of the younger brother who was the CO, I arranged to have a few last minute additions made to the van's ignition and heating systems and was waiting outside the jail when the prisoners pulled out. I followed them at a slight distance as they got onto the rural highway and headed north. At about the half way point, when I assumed everyone was good and relaxed, I activated first the gas in the heater system. My equipment guy who was an absolute genius when it came to anything with chemicals or narcotics had made up a remote control activated package of a Fentanyl-derived knock out gas. The trick was that you had to figure in the square feet of the area it would be dispensed in, combined with the approximate weights and sexes of your targets. Fentanyl was some stuff that the Russians had used and was very effective if used properly. Unfortunately, it was also fatal is used incorrectly and I couldn't have my guys or the guards that were transporting them dying before I got to them. I then hit the kill switch that had been placed on the ignition prior to their departure and as the vehicle began to slow down the driver instinctively pulled off to the side of the road passing out from the odorless gas a few moments later. I pulled in behind them and waited a few more minutes to insure that all of the occupants were out cold. Shutting off my lights, I approached the now quiet prison van. I opened the door and slid the driver out pulling him safely to the side of the road. I repeated the action with the passenger and was loading the small scooter I had purchased to come back and get my truck when I noticed five prisoners, not four as I had planned. I found the transport manifest and learned that the odd man out was some young kid who had been popped for check forgery and was added to the shuttle at the last moment. My first thought was just to kill him and dump him in the field but for some reason, and I don't know why, I had a brief moment of sympathy and began to pull him from the rear of the vehicle. All of a sudden his eyes opened and he freaked the fuck out, grabbing me by my collar and attempting to fight me off. I told him to chill out and that I wasn't going to hurt him but he still kept fighting me. I'd had enough and I slammed him straight into the jaw with a closed palm strike as he quickly lost consciousness. I laid him out on the grass next to the unconscious guards and tried to straighten myself up as I noticed that during our fight he had ripped my shirt down on the left side, and my bird tattoo was now clearly visible. I knew the gas would make the victims memory of the event cloudy at best and I felt that I was still safe, and as Ii was dark out I was pretty confident that the kid would never remember my face or anything else. I started the van and drove off about five miles, and then quickly drove the scooter back to retrieve my truck before any of them woke up. I parked the truck in a gas station that was closed for the night and headed for the farm.

When I got to my place I drove the van down into the barn, gave each of the thugs a shot of morphine to keep them relaxed, and headed back to get the truck. By now it was almost sun up and as I parked the pickup in the big barn I began o make preparations for my guests. They were all still doped up but were now waking to the fact that they weren't headed to prison. I had pulled them all out while still unconscious and had them securely chained ten feet apart to a wooden wall of one of the many horse stalls. I had made many advance preparations, one of which was to purchase four straight jackets like they used in mental hospitals for unruly patients, and the boys were all wrapped up snug as a bug in their new coats. I had taped their mouths securely so while they could watch me work and wonder what I was doing, they could ask no questions. I went to work pulling all of the bench seats out of the van and bolting eye hooks at strategic intervals. I cut a 24 by 24 square hole in the roof of the transport, and finally installed four small cameras with audio and video capability. Next, one at a time I moved the rapists back into the now modified vehicle. As I secured their hands and feet to the eye hooks I attached an IV with a ten foot tube extension to each man as well as a CO_2 operated four shot adrenalin pack that was duct taped to their upper left leg. When I had them all prepped and locked back inside I drove my newly constructed laboratory on wheels down into the pit I had dug behind the barn. After a couple hours of sleep I began to construct a lincoln log type bonfire over the large hole with my friends sitting inside the van wondering what the hell I was doing. I had killed some time over the past few days cutting up large logs that were in ready supply in the forest at the back of the property and with the help of the excavator I easily built a ready to go bonfire that any college fraternity would have been proud of. I made it 8 feet high as I wanted it to do what I needed it to, but not attract too much attention.

I started to work that afternoon as I introduced myself to the occupants of the semi buried van over the speaker I had installed in the cab area. As I began to spell it out for them I could see from my cameras that all but Big Time had began to have a really concerned look on their faces. I think the gang leader really did not give a damn but I knew I could change his mind. I dropped a canister of CS gas into the square hole in the ceiling and watched as they all began to jerk about with spit and snot flowing freely from their chemically burning faces. Even Big Time couldn't keep his composure during the tear gas, nobody can. I let them sit for a while and as I had removed the tape from their mouths prior to beginning I could now hear them plead for their lives, whining like a bunch of little bitches, even the tough guy, Big Time. I spoke to them on speaker again explaining that I was aware that they liked to put their cigars out in peoples flesh and that I was now going to allow them the pleasure of having some idea of what that felt like as I dropped the uncovered bee hive down the hole in the roof. The bees went crazy and I had put a piece of sheet metal over the hole so they had nowhere to go and nothing to do but take their anger out on anyone in the enclosed space. They all looked like they were being electrocuted as the bees stung them each a thousand times. I gave them a few minutes and then activated the first of the adrenalin shots I would remotely administer to keep them from dying to soon. I watched as their faces began to swell from the stings and gave them a second shot of adrenalin. After about 15 minutes I jerked the cover from the hole and dropped a small smoke bomb into it to accelerate the buzzing swarms exit. After the smoke cleared I watched the camera again as the occupants were now in various stages of shock and bewilderment. I could smell that some had shit themselves and all had pissed the front of their jail trousers and had multiple welts clearly visible on any area of exposed flesh. I let them ponder their position for another hour without any words coming out of the speaker. Just when they seemed to be composing themselves again I said hello as the mere sound of my voice sent them all once again into a very visible panic. I asked them if they enjoyed campfires and they all frantically looked around at each other as I lit the one I had built directly above them...

I was able to observe and record the end of the ordeal as the flames above began to cook the occupants below. First their hair began to catch fire and then the skin on their faces began to blister from the increasing heat. Within 20 minutes they were all incinerated and the fire above, combined with the weight of the heavy logs, was beginning to compress the van and its occupants into what would become an 18 inch pile of ashes in the bottom of the pit by morning. The next day I filled in the hole, topping it with rich black soil, premium grass seed, and plenty of mulch to insure rapid growth. Over the next week I mailed the DVD of my work to the requesting parties, sterilized the farm, and watered the grass seed a few more times. When the day of my departure finally came I called the rental company to come pick up their excavating equipment. After they left I drove my pickup to the airport, removing the plates before boarding my flight back to Grand Rapids. I had been paid in advance, and a pretty hefty sum at that, so as the plane took off I started to think about how to invest my pay. I thought about more real estate but real estate was kind of boring. Maybe a horse ranch I thought. Isis had always loved horses and in spite of having to work the majority of the past few weeks, I found that I really enjoyed being on a farm.

———————————————

Nineteen

By rule most people don't associate humor with death, nor would they expect those intricately involved with it to be laughing at times while they performed their duty, but Kevin "Ferg" Ferguson was an exception to the rules in more ways than one. Ferg always looked at things from a slightly different point of view and I always thought that was how he dealt with what he dealt with in the funeral business. I have no problem being the person that sends you to the undertaker, and I have no qualms or reservations about how I send you there, but there is just no way I could do what they do once you get there. Maybe it's just a bit too intimate. These were the people who got you ready for the last trip, so to speak, and even though you're not going to be giving any feedback, it would just be too personal for me. I wouldn't know how to act around someone I had to embalm, reconstruct, or even wash and dress. I know this sounds ridiculous coming from a hit man, but no thanks, it would just give me the creeps.

Being in the business I was in I had had many a deep conversation with Ferg. We talked plenty about the details of the job, the weird stuff that happens along the way, or just the plain fucked up reality that we both experienced in our line of work. More often than not though, we talked about food, music, and those people who we had yet to get to know on a professional basis. We also smoked a lot of pot. For me I liked the creative and relaxation aspects of it. It made me go outside of myself and that was a good place to be at times. It's not like I had post traumatic stress or anything similar. As I've already mentioned the job never bothered me in that regard. It was just nice to have a vacation from reality. With Ferg it was the same way and sometimes I thought he needed it even more. I killed people who had earned it but what about having to handle those who hadn't. Ferg talked to me once about embalming babies or stillborns. As usual he had a slight sense of humor about it but I could see it was just a front. Dead kids bother everybody and it bothered Ferg but he still had a job to do. I asked him how he did it, and I meant mentally, but he must have thought I meant the actual mechanics of it. He said you pickle them. This struck me as one of the weirdest things I had ever heard and I'd heard a lot of weird stuff in my life, but being that it was Ferg, and I knew Ferg, I figured there must be a soft side to his statement. He explained that really the only effective way to perform the process, due to their size, age, and lack of anatomical development, was to, in a sense, pickle them. He explained that you simply placed them in a five-gallon bucket of formaldehyde and the submersion would accomplish what normally required invasive and multiple injections on adults. We didn't talk a lot more about it as it was not a comfortable subject for either one of us.

Ferg owned two funeral homes in Detroit, one in the inner city, and one in a more upscale part of town. He actually lived in a swanked out pad above the inner city location and when I would visit him man did we hear and see some crazy shit. He had a pretty sweet place, all decked out and professionally decorated but with a touch of Ferg thrown in. For me it was like a cross between Graceland, a college dorm, and an Andy Warhol studio. He had this huge slate pool table that cost six grand, two pinball machines, the biggest TV money could buy, a kitchen with every gadget and appliance you could think of, a liquor cabinet that would make most bars pale in comparison, red velvet wall paper in every room, a bathroom the size of most living rooms, with a huge bath tub surrounded by fake statues and plants, neon everywhere, and a huge veranda on the back end that looked out over the neighborhood. Many nights we sat on the veranda smoking a joint and listened to the sounds of inner Detroit before we headed out to look for some action. We'd hear gunshots almost every time, hear sirens at varying distances, and unfortunately also always smell dog shit, as Ferg had two pit bulls that he let out on the veranda to do their business, and rarely cleaned it up.

One night once again we got woken up in the wee hours of the morning by some screaming crack head using the public pay phone on the sidewalk below the apartment. The next morning

Ferg called the phone company explaining the situation and asking them to please remove the phone as it presented a clear nuisance. They explained that it was on a public sidewalk, generated income, and wasn't going anywhere. He thanked them as he hung up the phone saying to himself "we'll see about that..." The next night he put on a pair of rubber gloves, scooped up a handful of warm dog shit, and proceeded to walk down stairs and smear it on the earpiece part of the pay phone. When he came back up I asked him what he did and as he poured us a couple of Jim Beam and diet cokes said "let's go sit on the deck, were gonna hear some fireworks." Sure enough about twenty minutes later the first victim walked up to use the phone, resting the phone between their ear and shoulder as they dialed. We could hear them yell as they realized that they now had dog shit all over their ear and shirt, slamming the phone loudly on the metal base and screaming about the shit. After a few hours, and a few more victims smashing the phone out of anger, the phone became no longer operable and was never replaced Problem solved...

Ferg loved to cook, and loved to eat, and he was pretty good at both. He knew all of the local mom and pop shops with food you couldn't get anywhere else; a lot of Italian, soul food, Greek, polish, you name it, he knew it. One of our favorites was Guido's Red Cloth, or just Guido's as the locals called it. It was a tiny Italian joint, owned by the same family forever, with 12 tables and an ever present smell of roasting garlic and simmering pots of marinara. The owner openly bragged about the fact that every sauce, strand of pasta, loaf of bread, and sugar dusted cannoli was made right there, and he had every right to brag; it was amazing. Ferg said that the local capos did some business here but we avoided any further conversation on this for both professional reasons and personal choice on both sides. He worked with them. I had done work for them, but this wasn't something you talked about in such close quarters and especially over a plate of made-from-scratch carbonara, I mean why wreck such a great meal with shop talk. We occasionally visited Lyles Corned Beef where they roasted their own corned beef and polish ham, and sliced it off hot, in huge portions, onto homemade bread with homemade sweet pickles and horseradish on the side. We would hit Greektown and gamble for hours, eventually hitting some off the path diner for shots of ouzo, flaming saganaki, and huge platters of mixed gyro meat, with rice and dolmas, olives and pickled turnips on the side, and warm Greek bread to wrap it all up in. We had a blast, and this was all before we even considered looking for some female companionship to end the night. We both liked sex and loved women, but sometimes I think we loved our friendship even more. More often than not by the time either one of us had thought of the opposite sex, we were either too full, to stoned, or too tired, to even pursue it with any real enthusiasm.

As I said before Ferg did some work for the local mob. I don't know exactly what and I didn't need to. One of the smartest things we had going for us was to never work together. I had referred him, and he had referred me, but we never mixed the two, ever. Ferg was involved in more shit than I could begin to talk about, probably the most obvious of which was making bodies disappear, and this is a big business, especially in Detroit. I remember one time when he visited he talked about having some of the local bosses wanting him to open a crematorium under his name, but with their money and I assume unlimited access. He asked me what I thought and I tried to steer him away from it. Being involved with the big boys was always something you needed to respect and handle with kid gloves. They don't play, and they don't tolerate mistakes. I figured he was making enough cash already, why go any deeper? I gave him my opinion and let it go. The next time I saw him he was driving a $60,000 Lincoln Navigator and buying a condo in south Florida. So much for advice.

The funeral business and the mob was only one part of his operation. He was well known as a reconstruction specialist and would subcontract his talents to other funeral homes with the latitude to name his own fee. Violence produces devastating results to the human body and on many occasions the loved ones left behind would insist on an open casket even when common sense, the human eye, and the funeral director were telling them not to. Here's where Kevin came in to the picture. Let's say you have some dude that just took an AK-47 blast to the face. If there is anything left of the skull and head you can rebuilt them, to a degree. Kevin would get called in and would tell the family to bring in a dozen recent pictures of the deceased. He then spent the next day working his magic with trimmings from a wig, chicken wire, and paper mache. The end result still looked fake as hell and he never denied it, but if an open coffin is what they wanted, Ferg could make it happen. He was friendly with the local vice squad, gang bangers, dealers, and outlaw motorcycle groups. I never could figure the cop thing, not to say that there aren't a few who are borderline ok, but people like us just didn't hang out with cops, but I figured whatever, he's a grown up and it's his choice. The gang bangers made sense, they were great customers. These guys were getting shot on a regular basis and they had cash. In the gang life the biggest tribute that you can have, and the last, is your funeral. If you're anybody of any prominence in the group they will drop a shit load of dough to show the world that they're sending you out proper. Ferg could really schmooze these dudes and play the respect your homies angle to the tee. He would sell them the most expensive, gaudy ass casket in his inventory. He told me once that when he had some piece of crap, dead Elvis looking box that no one would buy and he wanted to get rid of it, he would sell it to the gang bangers. He would talk about it like it was a classic car, a one of a kind, and the only thing good enough for burying their boy in, and he would up the price by half to prove his point. They may have been street smart, but they were dumb as fuck when it came to this, and he took all of their money, every time.

The dealers were a good angle as well, especially if you liked quality, which he did, but I think he just liked rubbing elbows with the rough boys, and he hated being bored, so his choice of associations was somewhat inevitable. Ferg always had good pot and great stories, and his friends were a constant source of both. Dealers in any part of the world see their share of interesting stuff but Detroit is one big, bad dog, and big dogs have big teeth, so inevitably the dog bite stories are going to be bigger too. The dealers supplied the hookers, the hookers supplied the johns, and the pimps watched it all and talked shit about the eventual outcome afterwards to maintain their street cred, but the bikers were the craziest of all of them.

The bikers ran dope, guns, hookers, chop shops, protection rackets, and anything else they could make money on, and Ferg could see a money making opportunity from a mile away. He already had the trust of the dealers. The dealers had the stuff the bikers wanted, and the bikers had the stuff the dealers wanted, and they all loved Ferg. Eventually it was just a matter introductions and establishing everybody's cut. Ferg received a small percentage for being the middle man but I think his main motivation was in having the connections, and the fact that everybody knew he had those connections. It was great insurance. I mean here you have a dude who is tight with bikers, dealers, mob guys ranging from simple leg breakers, all the way up to the bosses themselves. Who in their right mind is ever going to even think about fucking with a guy like that? He was tough enough, and we had been in a couple of situations in the past were I saw him in action, but now he didn't need to even worry about it, his reputation and friendships kept any potential problems from even beginning.

Most of the time we mainly cruised Detroit, gambled, ate out, or occasionally went to a concert or Red Wings game, but this one night Ferg wanted to take me to a blind pig, owned and operated by a local outlaw motorcycle club. The group had many business interests and one of those was illegal drinking establishments, or blind pigs as they were called. Ferg assured me, brother you have nothing to worry about, and we are going to have a good time tonight! This was unfamiliar territory for me, but I was going in with Ferg so I figured everything would be cool and we'd just have some drinks and leave. Turns out that was about as far from the truth as I could have imagined.

We walk in and immediately all of these huge, tattooed, bearded, mean looking bikers were all over us, but they were happy and laughing. Little Jimmy, the boss, came up and gave Ferg a big hug like he was a long lost brother. Everybody was slapping his back or hugging him like it was a friggin' fraternity bash. Nobody was even looking at me and I was just fine with that. These types of get together were definitely not my thing, but I wasn't going to be rude or stupid so I just smiled and kept my mouth shut. Eventually he got around to introducing me as a good friend and that was all he had to say. We were seated at Little Jimmy's private table, told that are money was no good, and we would not be paying for anything the entire night, and we were offered whatever you can imagine, all on the house; blow, weed, liquor, strippers, you name it. We ended up smoking a joint of some stuff the bikers bragged about as their pride and joy, and as it turns out I was going to need something to keep me calm, so it was a good thing I had. As the night got older the party got wilder and louder, and all of a sudden Little Jimmy got this really serious look on his face and leaned over to say something to one of his main dudes. I see them watching this guy up at the bar and I notice that, besides Ferg and I, he's the only guy not wearing biker leather or a patch of any kind. Little Jimmy and his sergeant at arms, Billy "Big Bear" Wilson started plotting something and the only thing I could surmise was that it involved the dude at the bar, and it was not in his favor. Meanwhile Ferg is oblivious to it all. He's got a bourbon and coke in one hand, a cigarette in the other, one stripper on his lap, and one dancing around him waving her ass in his face. He didn't have a care in the world.

All of a sudden Little Jimmy and Big Bear walk up to the dude at the bar. Everyone else just moved away and went on about their business. You could immediately see the fear in his eyes and feel the tension in the air. Turns out this guy had owed

Little Jimmy five grand for some time now, and not only hadn't he paid back the debt, but he was going around town telling people that Little Jimmy was a punk, fuck Little Jimmy, and I'm not paying that pussy jack shit. Apparently, he hadn't familiarized himself with who Little Jimmy actually was before letting his mouth run and he had just walked into the one bar in town that Little Jimmy not only owned, but could do anything he wanted without ever worrying about any cooperating witnesses. Little Jimmy smiled and said so, I hear you don't plan on paying me and consider yourself somewhat of a bad ass. The guy stuttered and stammered and said he hadn't said anything and was just having a hard time getting the cash but he would, and he would pay Little Jimmy just as quick as he could. Little Jimmy just smiled and let the guy sweat and shake for a minute. He turned around and told big bear to give him a gun, which he did. Little Jimmy, still smiling, turned back around and quickly put the automatic right up to the side of the guys head, and said next time find out who you're dealing with before you open your mouth, and pulled the trigger. I thought the dude was going to collapse from fear or shit his pants, which it turns out he did, but the gun hadn't fired. Apparently, the shell was a dud, or the gun had some kind of malfunction, but it didn't fire. Everybody kind of froze in disbelief at what had just happened except Ferg who was still laughing and drinking, and enjoying the girls. This guy should have had his brains and blood all over the wall but instead was still breathing. Little Jimmy later told us that he was just amazed at what had happened. He had pulled guns on and shot plenty of guys in his day, but this was a first, and that was the only reason he made his next decision. Little Jimmy turned to another one of his guys and again said give me a gun and again, faced the dude at the bar. He said you are one lucky son of a bitch, but luck only goes so far then he shot him in the left foot, and this time the gun worked. The guy dropped on the floor bleeding a screaming, and Little Jimmy looked down at him and said you have 24 hours to pay me and once you do don't ever let me see your fucking face in Detroit again.

Little Jimmy came over to where Ferg and I were seated, sat down, took a sip of his drink, sat it on the table and looked me right in the eye and said did you see that crazy shit? I took a sip out of my drink, sat it back down on the table, and calmly replied "what crazy shit?" Little Jimmy laughed with a slight, almost mischievous grin, and said "good answer".

Twenty

Dr. William Halter was a respected and for all visual purposes, a successful child psychiatrist. He had a small practice in a money part of town where, along with his two partners, he served the local depressed and delusional population. It can't be said that he was all bad, just by default he had helped a few kids along the way, but like many others he had gotten greedy and lax. He went into the psychiatric field with the common save the world mentality but like so many high paying professions doing the right thing was soon replaced by show me the money.

Suzy Patrelli was eight years old and having some difficulty in school and at home with her mother Michelle. The issue was with mom and her lack of parenting skills, combined with a habit of bad wine and anti depressants but mom had a hard time accepting this so, instead she chose to label the little girl as the problem. Being that she was the custodial parent she pretty much had free reign to cart the girl all over town, seeking out sympathetic clinicians and trying to obtain any diagnosis she could get, all the way from ADHD to pervasive mood disorder. The child had been to 17 different doctors in the course of two years and in every instance her father would eventually be informed of the appointments after the fact, make his own appointment with the doctor, and once again defeat her mother's efforts to achieve yet another exaggerated diagnosis. Suzy did have some obvious over activity in the talking department and after thorough examination her dad agreed that his little girl probably was ADHD, and she began taking the medication Strattera for her condition. Things had been on the upswing and Suzy was doing great and loving life that is until Dr. William Halter entered the picture.

Dr. Halter had a long history of flinging out multiple prescriptions. He was the one doctor in the local psychiatry community who was guaranteed to write a script and was well known for it. This may have been acceptable for the elitist parents who were just seeking out a quick pill fix to throw a blanket over the real issues with their kids but that wouldn't save his ass in the end. When Suzy first came to see the doctor her dad was once again not informed or involved. As usual mom began to paint a picture of all of the problems that poor the little girl was having. Mom liked to go on the internet prior to any appointment and search for signs and symptoms of whatever diagnosis she was trying to obtain. By doing so she literally knew what to say and knew how to subtly rig the game in her favor. The mom would say well she does this and she does this and sometimes she does this and this. I don't know what to make of it, but I'm really concerned knowing full well that the words or descriptions she had used would trigger pre programmed alarms in a doctor's analytical mind. The doctor nodded, and nodded, and complemented mom for her carrying and concern over her daughter. He lackadaisically suggested an additional diagnosis of depression which was exactly what mom had been hoping for, and of course recommended additional medication, which mom readily agreed with and thanked him profusely for both his help and understanding. What a fucking dumb ass. As I got to know a bit about more the good doctor I secretly wished I could have played poker against him just once before I had to kill him. I could have retired early...

Suzy and her mom had recently moved and with the new address came a new pharmacy as well, one that had no records showing the young girl currently taking Strattera. Dr. Halters, apparently without screening the mom first for current medications, wrote a script for Zoloft to help with the little girls depression. Within a week the Suzy began complaining of odd thoughts, sleeplessness, and abdominal pain, for which her flake of a mom would just tell her to take a nap, or make herself a cup of hot cocoa, while she herself sat on the back porch smoking off brand cigarettes and drinking more bad wine. One morning after having complained about her increasing side effects to her mother for almost three weeks, Suzy didn't wake up. The official diagnosis was serotonin syndrome, which was relatively new but not unheard of to the psychiatric community. The eight year old girl was laid to rest in a quiet cemetery on a Sunday morning, with her completely distraught father looking on through his blood shot eyes wondering why his little girl had been taken from the world so soon. After receiving the autopsy results and a toxicology report which the mother had attempted to keep from him, he soon had an answer to his painful question. Suzy's dad was an average working man with some very un-average friends and associations. Of these were a couple of Albanian brothers who ran a local laundry and dry cleaning service, but were also involved in some very nasty business on the side. They were all part of a group that played Texas Holdem on Monday nights and after having avoided the weekly game while mourning his daughter, Suzy's dad decided to join his friends in hopes of getting his mind off the recent loss. The cognac was flowing and with it eventually his own tears. He excused himself to go outside and one of the brothers followed him to offer his support. As they stood in the cold night air he began to explain to his foreign friend what had happened to his only child. It didn't have to happen, that was the hardest part. If the fucking shrink had performed just a little due diligence, or had given the father's input just a little more than dismissive thought, or had paid less attention to his own inflated ego, his little girl would still be alive. As the father continued the Albanian could feel his own anger rise up. He had three children, as did his brother, and he had complete loathing for anyone who did not consider a child's innocence. He had nothing but cold fury for someone who had taken it away. He explained to the father that, with his permission, there was something that could be done about it. Suzy's dad didn't know what he meant at first and as his friend loosely explained the solution he said that he would have to give it more consideration and in a less intoxicated state. He thanked his friend for his support and agreed to contact him with in the week with his answer. Five days later I got a phone call.

I met with the brothers and after they explained the situation negotiated a fee for my services. They had a few curious requests but this didn't bother me. It made the whole thing a bit more interesting and increased my pay which they didn't have any problem with. Dr. Halters lived in a gated community with a halfway decent alarm system. It presented a little challenge but nothing I couldn't handle and within a week I had bugged his home office, car, private practice, and his personal line at work. I followed him a little but most of what I needed to know I easily gained from the wire taps. After a week and a half I began to form a plan but this time I would need a little help. I had all sorts of friends from my work and my travels and one in particular was a sex for hire coordinator, or pimp as most people viewed him, with some high-end girls and clientele. I asked him how clean his girls were and he assured me that they were all top shelf. I told him that I needed one who was bottom shelf and he asked me what I meant. I explained that I needed a girl with a venereal disease, and preferably herpes. He protested at first claiming that he didn't know anyone like that but I knew it was bullshit. If you fuck for a living you run the risk of catching something along the way. Condoms are great but they certainly aren't fool proof and we both knew it. Finally he confided that he had one of his girls that had herpes, but that she kept it well within control or at least as much as possible. She had monthly attacks and sometimes less frequently, but the one thing I knew about the disease was that stress increases the likely hood of an outbreak. I asked him how she looked and told him she had to be white as well. Dr. Halters, as I had come to find out, liked strange pussy, but he didn't do black girls or anyone with so much as a good tan. My friend told me that this girl was white as buttermilk and college educated to boot. I told him that I needed her to have an outbreak in the next week and asked if he could think of a way to stress her out. I hated to do this to a working girl who hadn't done anything to me, but I had a job to do and I needed her help. The pimp assured me that in the next few days he would most definitely "stress the bitch out."

The good doctor liked to stop at a classy seafood restaurant named "Leo's" on his way home every night. He always ordered a top shelf martini and some type of light appetizer. If he actually met some suitable female companionship, and he didn't seem that particular, he would call the wife at home and explain to her that he had another emergency call from the office and he would be late getting home. He always finished the call by telling her that he loved her and to kiss the kids goodnight, after which he would ask for the check as he ushered his new found acquaintance to a local hotel. Our girl was sitting at the bar the next week on a night that he showed up. They quickly engaged in conversation as she ordered more drinks, flirted with him lightly, and tossed him an occasional compliment. I was watching the whole thing from an adjacent table and I could tell his dick must have been getting as hard as Chinese arithmetic from her faithful doting. After several martinis and a few hours of relaxing, once again he picked up his phone. I paid my bill and was waiting in the parking lot as they headed down the road to his favorite hotel. When they got there the girl sent him to the store to get some more booze. He protested a little but he wanted some action and off he went. I knocked on the door after he left and quickly installed a couple of audio rigged hidden cameras to catch it all. I was sitting in my car when he raced back into the parking lot and as he ran up the shabby stairs to the hotel room I was afraid he might fall and break his neck, and keep me from having all of the fun I had planned. He was as big of a freak as I had thought and had the call girl do everything from whipping his bare buttocks with the wire from a bedside lamp, to pissing on him after she came. I videoed every bit of it and watched him drive away in the early hours of the next morning with a new and unknown gift of herpes now actively living in his genitals.

The very next night his children left to enjoy the free premier movie tickets they had won from a local contest that they had never actually entered. When the doctor got home his wife was already buttered up from the huge bouquet of her favorite flowers that had arrived late that afternoon, and which he had no memory of ordering but assumed his secretary had sent, covering his ass for whatever reason. A box of her favorite chocolates were sitting open and half eaten on the coffee table in the huge living room. She was nestled comfortably under a blanket, wearing nothing but a smile and even though the doc was pretty worn out from the night before, in light of the current picture before him knew he would have to put out, like it or not. After they finished he went off to the master bedroom to take a long shower, as his wife rested on the warm couch watching her favorite show and completely unaware that her loving husband had just given her the gift that keeps on giving. Next, I paid cash for some pretty bad bondage magazines from a local XXX and wrapped them precisely in brown wrapping paper exactly as they would have appeared prior to being shipped to a loyal subscriber. The only modification was a seemingly innocent tear in the packaging that easily revealed the nature of the contents to anyone taking a cursory look. I had made up a label addressing the publications to William Halters and placed the magazines in the mailbox just before sunrise knowing that the postman would just assume they had been left from the day before and simply add to the stack with bills and junk mail. His wife was in for her first surprise when she checked the mail that day. The porn mags would be hard enough for him to explain, but when his wife broke out in herpes sores a few weeks later and had it confirmed by her physician, her first phone call was to the best divorce lawyer in town.

Doc's world had been turned upside down and he quickly began spending more and more time at his favorite watering hole and self medicating with Ativan from his office supplied samples. I saddled up next to him at the bar one night and after some light talk told him that he didn't look so good. He needed a friend and I provided one as I sympathized with his self imposed plight. He had been living in hotels since his wife had him physically removed from their home and I think this hit him as hard as anything. I told him that I had a nice condo with two bedrooms and that I was hardly ever there as I traveled on business often. He declined at first but two nights later asked me if my offer was still good. I smiled and said it sure is my friend. He moved his stuff in the next day and insisted on paying me for his stay. I told him no at first but then accepted a thousand bucks and thanked him for his generosity. He began to tell me that he had no idea what had happened to him but he was beginning to think that someone had set it all up. I laughed at the possibility but told him that if he really believed it I knew some guys that might be able to help him find out who. He later asked me if I was serious and I agreed that I was. He asked about possible costs and I explained that I wasn't really that familiar with this type of thing but I supposed I could find out. A few days later I told him that my friend had explained to me that for ten grand they could find out but for thirty they could offer him some payback. He asked about payment and I explained that these matters were always handled with cash, preferably hundred dollar bills. Being both rich, paranoid, and pissed off, he came home the next day with three hundred and fifty-one hundred dollar bills fresh from the bank. He told me the extra five was to make sure they did a good job. I assured him they would.

He stopped going out as much preferring to drink from the well stocked bar in the condo I had rented on a six month lease the week before I offered him a room. One night later that week we had been watching a movie about some hit man from New York, as he excused himself to take a shower. His scotch and water sat waiting for him to return on the table next to his chair. When he came back he said he was feeling much better and asked if I had heard any progress as I said not yet, but I'm sure you'll know the truth very soon. An hour later the double dose of Strattera and Zoloft I had dumped into his scotch began to take effect. He said he didn't feel too good and was swaying slightly from side to side in his big easy chair. He complained of stomach pain and I came around to sit in front of him as his problems grew. I said maybe now you know how little Suzy felt. He just stared at me for a few minutes as the reality of his situation finally hit him.

I leaned forward and said I told you you'd know the truth very soon, didn't I.

I forced him to swallow a handful of Ativan and he was barely able to resist as I made him wash it down with some more scotch direct from the bottle. When the house cleaning lady showed up a few days later she found both the body and the suicide note that had been typed on the good doctors own laptop, and the signature at the bottom was a perfect match. In his letter he professed his guilt for both killing the little girl with his lack of professional diligence. He further professed his self loathing over his sexual malfeasance along with some other stuff he actually never did. Suzy's mother sued the estate and settled out of court. She never would have offered a nickel to the father but her lawyer explained that even though he didn't want any money, legally he was entitled to it. She would be better off if she simply made a good faith gesture which the father reluctantly accepted. One year later with an ample supply of money to feed her own alcohol and drug habit she drowned in her own bathtub. With what she had endured in the past year the easy and official conclusion was suicide. The thirty five grand that the doctor had paid me helped to make it look that way.

Twenty-One

The phone rang and as I looked at the caller ID I could see it was my brother who I hadn't talked with in over a month. What's up! I excitedly asked. With my recent packed work load I was greatly looking forward to a light hearted conversation with someone I loved. I thought maybe it was just me, or perhaps he was simply tired, but Diamo's voice sounded faded and worn. I didn't give it much thought as we caught up on life, our wives, mom and dad, and when Isis and I were going to have babies. I said that it would be sooner than later and as he told me to hurry it up it seemed like his voice carried an urgency it normally did not. He spoke a little of his job, and I assumed he just didn't want to talk shop which I could completely understand. He started reminiscing about our child hood and then began talking about how much he loved his wife and kids. I occasionally had found myself homesick for Sicily in the past and again just assumed that the same was true for him. He said that he had to ask me a very important question and I said shoot. He asked me if anything ever happened to him if I would look out for his family after he was gone and I quickly found myself feeling a combination of insult, anger, and alarm. What the fuck do you mean asking me such a thing? You know, without question, that I would always look out for you or your family no matter what!! The air held a dead silence and I apologized for my outburst but this wasn't the kind of question you can ever be prepared for, and I was thinking what the hell. My brother's in better health than I am and a god-damn doctor on top of it. Considering the polar opposite of our chosen careers I always thought that if anything I would be the one presenting this question to him. Again, there was silence and for the first time in our lives I thought that I had really hurt my brother and I began to feel like a jerk but I still didn't know why he would ask me such a silly question.

Dominick I have cancer. The words hit me right in the chest and I pulled my phone away to look at it as I simply did not believe I had heard what just came out of it. I placed it back to my ear as I said what?" I have cancer, he repeated again and I felt my body go numb. I couldn't speak, I couldn't think, I couldn't do anything but sputter out a few barely understand-able sentences. We both paused for a few minutes and more than anything else I wished in that moment that I was standing in front of him and he had given me the news in person. I thought at least then I could hug him, or I could yell, or I could say bullshit, you're lying, and it would be so, but none of that was going to happen. He had been diagnosed three months ago and had begun radiation and chemo but they weren't having much success. I said well then let's go someplace better, whatever it costs I don't care, I'll pay for it, and he said Dominick, it's not money that the issue. I have plenty of that. I just have a form of cancer that is very hard to treat and I don't know how much time I have left. I hadn't cried since Angelia had passed but found myself now 2,000 miles from the person in the world that I had been closest to my entire life and I was completely helpless as the warm tears streamed down my face. We spoke for a while about options, both in America and in Europe. I asked him if his wife knew and he said had not told her yet. I was really pissed at him for this but I shut up. When you're going through a rough time you lean on those who love you. When their going through trouble they can lean on you, that's part of the deal, but he was a grown man and although he was my brother I had to at least try and respect the way he chose to handle the possibility of his potential mortality.

I told him I would fly out the next day and he told me to make it a week so as not to alarm his wife. I wanted to leave that night but I respected his wishes. When I got out there I found it very hard to act like nothing was wrong. Diamo made me promise to out of concern for his wife and kids and although it was one of the hardest things I'd ever faced, I kept it together as I had been asked. We went out to eat, visited some local sites, and pretty much acted like it was just a surprise vacation from Uncle Dominic. At night, after everyone had gone to bed, we sat up and divided our time between talking about our childhood and planning out what he needed to do just in case the cancer won. He already had plenty of life insurance along with various investments so finances would not be a problem. I offered to pay for the children's college but this had already been planned for in advance. The main thing he asked me to do was to be there for his wife and kids as he knew that if he died it would be devastating for all of them. I told him that he never, ever needed to ask me to do that. It was both my duty and my honor as his brother. I flew back home the next night but visited as much as possible in the coming months without trying to cause any alarm. When his wife asked me about my frequent visits of late I lied and told her that I was just taking some time off from business and wanted to catch up on lost time with her, Diamo, and the kids. Eventually he started to respond to the various treatments and one day he called me again but this time it was to let me know that he was now in remission and thanked me over and over for my support. As a single tear streamed down my face I said hey, that's what brothers do.

Twenty-Two

Sometimes the greatest friendships we'll ever have in this life come completely out of nowhere. I don't even remember how I got introduced to Tim, I know it started with needing my car fixed and looking for a good mechanic when I moved to Grand Rapids, the rest would be just boring details that really don't matter anyway.

Tim "The Mechanic" Pomorski had spent his early childhood in Greenup County Kentucky. Greenup County was pretty much known because of four things; The Taylor Brickyard, Graf Brothers Lumber, poverty, and some of the country's best moonshine. The Taylor Brickyard was the name given to both the local railway station and the McCall post office, and was all run by a man by the name of Clyde King. Nothing happened in the county without Clyde King saying so or getting a piece of it. We referred to it as the *hillbilly mafia*. It might have sounded like a cartoonish label but make no mistake it was run with the same level of efficiency and ruthlessness as anything you'd see in Sicily, and on some occasions even rougher. Life here was certain and uncertain. There were rules of existence just like anyplace else but the penalties for disregarding or breaking those rules was significantly amplified in a place like Greenup. A man in Mr. King's position simply could not afford to be taken lightly or allow any degree of flexibility in his rule, and based on his reputation, he didn't. If the person in violation simply needed to be shown a lesson a public ass whipping and a few days in the local hospital would suffice. If this didn't work there were plenty of places to bury a body in the abundant hillside and this fact was not lost on anyone. In the most extreme and sensitive cases the problem would just be cut into manageable pieces, packed into a whiskey barrel, topped with lye, and pushed off an outbound train somewhere far, far away where, by the time anyone might discover it, the local rodents and carnivores would have scattered the bones way too far apart for anyone to ever make any sense out of.

I had a theory about it all. In Sicily we had our share of poverty, hardship, corruption, and the lot, and this type of environment produces a certain mentality and toughness in its inhabitants. That's completely understandable but to me the big difference was the food, the weather, and the women. Greenup had some great local fare, gorgeous countryside, and fine country women, which I'm sure the locals were mighty proud of but to me there was nothing like what we had at home. Grits, Kentucky blue grass, and southern gals just couldn't compare with pasta, lemon trees, and Italian women.

Just like me life hadn't handed Tim anything for free and maybe that's why we got along so good. As a boy he used to have to go and roust his grand daddy from the whiskey shed on more than one occasion. Grandma had issued him and his brother the task of getting grandpa ready to go to church but there was only one problem, grandpa made good strong whiskey, liked to partake in his own product, and would drink to the point of delusional thoughts more often than not, so when Tim and his brother, 10 and 12 years old at the time, would attempt to do their duty and fetch grandpa, they were more often than not greeted on their approach by double aught buckshot from grandpa's 12 gauge. See, grandpa would get so drunk that even when he woke up he still had one helluva buzz going and was paranoid as hell to boot, about revenuers and thieves trying to steal his shine. He shot first and if he asked any questions at all, they would come much later. Tim described in great detail how it was basically like a military maneuver getting grandpa to go to church. For starters, like most moon shiners if he had a choice of going to church or tending his still, the still always won out. Who could blame him, I thought. The boys would dread Sunday mornings both the going to church part and the grand daddy wrestle that was sure to come with it. I asked him one time why they just didn't say no. I mean dealing with gun fire as opposed to hurting an old woman's feelings hardly seemed like a much of a quandary. Tim said the answer was simple, even with the trouble that grand pa was guaranteed to give, and the bruises, cuts and scrapes, and occasional shotgun pellet in the ass that came with it, grandma was still a lot scarier. The first time he and his brother were tasked to fetch their grand dad they simply tried to jump him in his drunken sleep. They soon learned that was a big mistake. Grand pappy had been running shine, cutting timber, and basically working his butt off since he was a young boy and even at 65 he was no easy target and still strong as a bull. He easily bounced them both off the walls of the wood shed, grabbed them both by the collar, and ceremoniously tossed them out the door and back down the hill they had just walked up. The following week on their second attempt they brought some rope and a wheel barrow, planning to hog tie his ass and cart him down the hill for grandma to deal with however she saw fit. As it ended up Tim and his brother again took an unholy ass whooping, got tied up in their own rope, wheeled down the hill by grandpa, and deposited on grandma's front porch with grandpa laughing to himself the entire time. The following week he said they finally got a little smarter and decided to borrow one of grandma's cast iron frying pans for the trip up the hill. Not sure if it was out of fear or simply with the intent of evening the score for the whooping they took earlier, but he said it worked.

They flanked the shed as opposed to walking up in plane site as they had done before. As they crept around the back of the shed, frying pan in hand, they looked through the window and saw grandpa snoring away in his favorite chair, oblivious to the world. As quietly as they could they slowly opened the window and slipped into the shed. Standing behind their sleeping grandpa they quickly realized they had yet another problem; they hadn't discussed who would smack grandpa with the pan. They were scared of grandma and scared of grandpa but they still loved him and thinking like children were more conscious of the pain of the act than the pain of not acting. Tim said he finally just thought fuck it, I'm not taken another ass whooping by grandpa or grandma. He grabbed the pan out of his brother's hand and laid old grandpa out on the floor with one hard smack to the back of the head. At first he thought he had killed him and that brought about all kinds of other worries, but this wasn't the first time the old man had been whacked and he started to slowly come around. At that point wisdom came to both boys and they hog tied old grandpa as tight as a sack full of rabid squirrels, loaded him in the wheel barrow, and brought him down the hill to their grinning and applauding grandmother.

At first I just figured Tim for a working man, a damn good mechanic, and an all around average Joe. While to some degree these are all accurate, the real Tim I was soon to find out was much more complex; as smart as any college professor, more so than most, well connected, and the kind of guy you wanted as your friend, not your enemy. Tim had a wonderful wife, and two charming daughters, and he dearly loved them all. He spent his free time, and their wasn't a lot of it, going to the girls school functions and after school dance activities, was quite active in the local community, and truly enjoyed the weekends with his wife and kids. He had other family but this was the heart of it and, as everyone knows, you always look out for your heart.

The first time I got an idea of what Tim could do was when these two dudes walked into his shop one day as I was waiting for my car to be fixed. I had been coming there for so long I pretty much made myself at home anytime I was there, and on many occasions other customers would incorrectly assume that I was an employee of the shop. Today was no different and I was in the office checking some shit out on the computer when these guys walked in. The smaller one asked for Tim and I just pointed over my shoulder towards the back of the shop without hardly looking up. After a few minutes I walked back into the shop to see how my car was doing and the two dudes that I had sent back were talking to Tim with their backs to me. Tim looked passed them and directly at me with a look I can't really describe but I knew it was serious and I knew he was pissed. I figured it was just some car bull shit and I wouldn't need to get involved but as I walked passed to grab my briefcase out of my back seat I noticed the small one displaying a gun in his waist band with a very angry look on his face. Apparently a former employee of Tim's had accepted thirty grand from them to customize a car and put in a sound system. Tim had no involvement in the deal but the guy had fled the city with these guys money in his pocket, and they were now demanding that he come up with the dough. He had tried to explain to them that he knew nothing about it but they weren't listening and were demanding that he pay them himself or face the consequences. They were some gang banger wannabe's with a slightly busy drug corner in the hood and must have thought they could walk in with their jail house tattoos and tough talk and Tim would just give them the cash. Man were they ever wrong. First off he didn't have thirty grand, but as he said later even if he had he sure as hell wouldn't have given it to these ghetto niggers. It might have gotten talked out but the small one came out and said that they had been watching the shop for a while and noticed that Tim's pretty blond wife and two beautiful daughters came to pick him up every day promptly at 6:30 pm. Maybe we can take our money out in trade off that pretty white pussy, course it'll take a while he said, as they both laughed at their joke. While they were laughing Lucky Larry was quietly walking up from behind and laid the short one out with a piece of pipe just as cold as a block of ice. The big dude turned to face their attacker and I quickly grabbed him from behind, as I pulled my nine millimeter and jammed it hard into his ribs and said don't even breath motherfucker. When shorty woke up in they were both standing upright with their wrists tightly bound by chains to an overhead beam in the paint booth of the shop. The booth had been built by Tim and Larry along with a very big furnace in the next room that they used to heat the shop in the winter months, and the booth was completely sound proof. This was not going to end well.

Lucky Larry as we liked to call him was a homeless dude that Tim had befriended some time ago. Larry was a good guy and although maybe not that smart in some areas was a work horse when it came to fixing cars. Tim always said that if Larry didn't know how to fix something all Tim had to do was explain it to him once and from then on he could do it perfectly every time. The main thing I admired about Larry was that he was loyal. He wasn't a Sicilian but I guess it just came natural to him. I think that because so many people had shit on him in his life when he finally found someone who actually cared about him he was like an old stray dog and would not only protect his friend but would never leave his side. Larry also had another very valuable attribute. He could follow orders without any emotion whatsoever, and these boys were about to find out what that would mean. We knew they weren't going anywhere but just in case Tim had posted Larry to watch over them as he and I went across the street for a cup of coffee and a slice of pie. As we left he promised to bring Larry back a piece of Dutch apple with ice cream and hot cocoa and Larry's eyes lit up like a little kid. As our coffee came Tim said so what now? I didn't really know what he meant and he explained how even though he considered us friends, I had now seen another side of his life and I just shrugged my shoulders as I took a sip of my drink and said Tim, it's no big deal. He laughed, looked me hard in the eyes, and said "no big deal" do you have any idea what were going to do to these two dudes. Now I laughed and said that I had a pretty good idea, but really didn't care. I went on to tell Tim that if they had said that about my wife and kids they would already be dead and I wouldn't have taken the time to play with them like you did. I wasn't trying to one up him or offend but I killed people quickly when the job called for it, and when it came to fucking with people I loved there was no grey area whatsoever. The pie came and it was so good I ordered two more to bring home to share with Isis later that night. I drained my coffee and asked Tim what I owed him for fixing my car as I had to get going. He looked at me for a second and said man you are one ice cold individual, and the car's on me this time. I thanked him for his gift and said only when I need to be, as I walked out the door with my two pieces of pie.

Twenty-Three

It had been a while since we had taken a vacation and with the cold of January making its presence well known I booked two tickets to Jamaica and packed the suntan lotion. I had been here a few times in the past and had always enjoyed the easy going spirit of the people who seemed to always carry a song in their step and a smile on their face. As we began our approach to the airport in Montego Bay you could look out the windows and see the blue and green Caribbean surf below. It was always a magical transformation for me in the past and I could tell that my wife was having the same experience as the big wheels of the plane hit the tarmac and we comfortably bounced to a stop. Fifteen minutes later we were in an air conditioned shuttle bus that would carry us on our hour and a half journey to Negril. I had stayed in Mo Bay before and it was alright if you wanted to party all night and sleep all day working on your tan. Ocho Rios was in the other direction and it was an okay place to visit but leaned quite heavily towards the all inclusive, eat until you explode, Hawaiian shirt wearing it's our anniversary crowd. For my interest you just couldn't beat Negril. For starters you got much better accommodations and service for half the cost of the tourist traps. Just as important if not more was its seclusion. As I said it was a good hour and a half bus trip and just by default this screened out over half the people. As we came around the corner of Seven Mile Beach I saw the crystal white sand lined for as far as you could see with tiki huts, small resorts, and hammocks with people lazily sipping on a cold drink without a care in the world.

We checked into our hotel and as I introduced us I gave my gifts to Carissa at the front desk. This was an old trick I had learned on my first visit that guaranteed you would have both great service and no hassles. If, when you made your reservations, you asked the person on the other line if they would like anything from the States you had a friend on staff before you even arrived. Today was no different as I handed over the Egyptian cotton sheets, coffee maker, and small case of Ivory soap to our smiling hostess. I had brought two large suitcases along with my big dive bag and one of the cases was completely full of trading items for the people of the island. The natives loved American sports t-shirts, ivory soap (for some odd reason), small packets of brilliantly colored glass beads, and any kind of cologne or perfume made in the states. I also had playing cards, bags of colored balloons, and tiny toy cars for the children as well as an ample supply of American dollars that I would use for tips and additional bartering power. As the main guard showed us to our room I handed him two $20 bills and asked him to keep an eye on our place during the visit. If we didn't have any problems I would repeat the process when we left and he knew it so it was just a small insurance policy to alleviate potential bullshit. The island mood struck us as soon as the door closed and after an hour of frolicking on the canopied king sized bed we were both very hungry, so down to the beach we headed. One thing they say about Jamaica is that everyone is on island time and they aren't kidding. Another guest had once explained to me with a smile that if you're the impatient kind you should probably place your lunch order when your finishing breakfast. It was lunch time and we ordered a mixed plate of jerked goat, garlic shrimp, rice and pea's, and fried plantains on the side. We grabbed a couple of cold red stripes from the bar and sat back in the beach chairs to wait for our food to cook. As we gazed out on the blue water I began to think of Sicily without palm trees. After a few minutes Isis said that it reminded her very much of Greece, but with no cliffs. It was just a wonderful moment and we didn't feel the need to talk much as we simply took in the smell of the ocean and the warm embrace of the tropical breeze. Our lunch arrived a while later and the cook had included a delicious salad of cabbage and mango, hearts of palm, with fresh lemon juice, and some type of spice that tasted a little like nutmeg and curry. Neither one of us could finish everything and as I left a generous tip we went for a stroll along the beach to help digest our food.

The next day we awoke to the calls of the local street kids hawking their wares of fruit, coconut bread, beef patties, and fresh squeezed juice in reused glass bottles that they carried in wooden crates that had been packed with a thin layer of chopped ice and were supported by a leather strap that draped around their young necks. They occasionally sold a type of soft cheese that went really well with the juice and coconut bread and I bought enough for our breakfast as I tipped the young entrepreneur with a crisp green $5 bill. He smiled with a few teeth missing and said respect mon as we fist bumped our clenches hands. I remembered my young days of hustling the streets as I smiled and agreed. Ya mon, respect I said and off he went to make his money. We went on boat rides and I dove a little which prompted Isis to swear that I was crazy. She had never been a fan of the ocean as she had been convinced as a young girl that as soon as you entered you would be eaten by either a shark or some mysterious sea creature. I laughed at her as I assured her that I had been scuba diving for many years and although I had swam with sharks on occasion, had never incurred so much as even a small problem. She still wasn't buying it and preferred to stay on the boat as she sipped on rum punch and danced to reggae with the other passengers. Night time was always an adventure and a revolving parade of drinking, dancing, and carousing among the single people with the ever present scent of ganja drifting in the tropical wind. We were sitting at the resorts beach side bar when these three Jamaican dudes came strolling up. I could sense trouble right off the bat and my instincts where confirmed as one of them began openly flirting with my wife. She smiled as she thanked him for the flattery but assured him that she was quite happily married as I smiled and tipped my glass in their direction. This should have been enough but the dude was either too stoned or too cocky to take a hint. He reached out and grabbed her wrist as he said you got no ring missy. If you married where's da ring? She pulled her arm back and I quickly got up and stood between them as I said hands off my friend. Like the lady said, she's married to me. He smiled and glanced around at his two other friends as he decided to challenge me and say that she deserved better if I could not even afford to buy her a ring. His friends both laughed at the insult and I was pondering their demise when the security guard I had tipped earlier grabbed my new acquaintance by the collar and easily spun him around, tapping his dark billy club on his shoulder as he said mon, if you want trouble I gonna give you some. The whole thing ended as quickly as it began and the lady killers decided to seek entertainment elsewhere. Isis was kind of shook up. In our homeland no one would ever have put their hands on a married women like that and she suddenly lost all affection for our host country for the night. As we walked back to our cabana I assured her it was no big deal as I began to think of how I would handle these guys if I had to deal with them again.

I went out on the front patio to smoke a joint as she drifted off to sleep inside. I wasn't sure if I would have to deal with them or not but one thing was for certain, I was out gunned already. You could not bring any weapons into the country and I knew for a fact that one or all of them carried at minimum a blade. The thought of having to even deal with this shit made me madder than the situation itself and then I remembered the shish ka bobs we had been served at the beach side grill just a few hours ago. I put on my shoes as I walked back down to the waterfront. When I got there sure enough the metal skewers were sitting next to the grill where the busy chef had left them to cool off. I looked around in the darkness as I took two and hid them in the waist band of my shorts. The next morning I let my wife sleep in as I went into town for a few items. I found a small hardware store where I was able to buy some cloth tape much like the type you rewrap tennis racquets with. I also bought two feet of thin steel cable along with two metal screw down clamps, a screw driver, and a roll of duct tape. On the short walk home I was offered every kind of drug under the sun and when a guy offered to sell me coke I sampled a small amount to insure its quality and paid him for a one gram foil that I stuffed into my back pocket.

The next night sure enough the assholes where back and my wife was immediately uncomfortable as they glared across the bar with lecherous smirks on their faces. I told her to go back to the room and she resisted at first wondering what I was going to do. I told her not to worry and just to go back and wait for me. I was a business man not a fighter I said, and she accepted my explanation and excused herself. After I was sure she was safe back in the room I made my way around the bar to offer my friends a drink. They all got looks of alarm on their faces as I said hey man it's no problem. I just want to party. They relaxed and accepted the free booze as I began ordering shots of the Jamaican 100 proof rum that the locals where so fond of. After a couple hours of rum and Red Stripes I asked about a dance club that I knew was right on the beach within a half mile walk. I said that I heard it had a lot of wild girls and I really wanted to check it out as I pulled out my Visa Platinum and said what do you say guys, drinks are on me? I knew that they all thought I was quite drunk as we had done seven shots of white rum, while washing it down with Red Stripes the entire time. What they didn't know was that the reason I had bought the coke was to keep me sober as I drank. They were all much more accustomed to the liquor than I was but I had been snorting small amounts of blow the whole time and was still very alert in spite of my exaggerated intoxication. I paid our tab as we all walked out onto the shining sand in the glistening moonlight. We talked and joked about girls as the mouthy one and I walked side by side just in front of the other two. I was wondering when they were going to try and jump me as I knew they would. I had the thin cable style garrote stuffed down the front of my pants with the two shanks I had made from the skewers and tape tucked inside the waist band of my pants. I looked around casually both in front of us and behind to make sure we didn't have any company. I told a joke that I knew would make them all laugh as I quickly spun around pulling the shanks and stabbing the two guys behind me repeatedly in the upper chest and abdomen. A shank, or anything like it such as an ice pick or a small round file, has much easier penetration than a knife. It's really just a matter of physics, but anyway I was able to stab them both six times before they had any idea what was going on. As they both dropped to the sand grasping at their wounds and gasping for breath, I turned to the last one as he started to run. I caught him quickly and took him to the ground as with one hand as I pulled out the garrote with the other. With the cable wrapped around his throat and his face buried in the sand he couldn't say a word as I thought to myself put your fucking hands on my wife will you? In minutes they were all very dead and I searched the surrounding beach for a small boat that the fisherman randomly left out every night. I dragged one down to the water as I loaded my drinking buddies into the hull. I popped in the oars and in 15 minutes found myself drifting off shore admiring the lights from the beach. I had told Isis that she didn't need to fear sharks in the ocean which was partially true. In the day time they can see and smell you from up to a mile away and will more often than not avoid human contact at all costs. Once the sun sets it's a different story all together. The same is true about how far away they can sense humans but night time is when they feed and I had a couple of nice meals just waiting for them. I stabbed all three of them a couple times in the carotid artery to insure that the ocean could receive plenty of predators attracting blood and threw them one at a time into the waiting water. As I rowed away from the partially submerged bodies I could see the water around them begin to churn with the feasting carnivores. Sharks are very greedy and they don't waste a bite so I knew the fellows would now become shark shit and would never hassle anybody ever again.

I jumped out of the boat just before the beach to look around for late night strollers and to let the warm salt water wash any blood from my clothes. I splashed a few buckets inside of the boat for the same reason and satisfied I was both safe and clean, pulled the small fishing vessel back up to its original spot. When I got back to our resort the security guard was sitting at the bar with only a few late night guests and had apparently seen me walk off with the trouble makers from last night. He asked me where my buddies where and I shook my head as I said I don't know, chasing women I guess? He smiled slightly and asked if I had gone for a swim. I agreed that I had and he just stared at me for a moment, turning around to look at the water, and said four men left, but only one came back... In my country we would call this a coincidence. What would they call it in America? As the bartender brought me a cold beer I took a quick sip, set it on the bar knowing that there was no evidence and that nobody cared, especially not the guard as I said "In my country they would say don't fuck with another man's wife."

One week after we got back Isis announced with a smile that I was going to be a father.

Twenty-Four

You still in the business, Tim said. That depends on which business you're talking about I replied. I had sold Hero's a while back and I highly doubted he was looking for someone to cater a birthday party but figured I'd find out the answer soon enough. I had stopped by the shop to have my mechanic friend check out the four wheel drive on my steel blue Jeep Commander. I loved my ride but the front end had been acting a little out of whack lately and I wanted to address it before I ended up in a ditch somewhere out in BFE. Tim looked up from the Jeep for a second and said the payback business. I grabbed an old chair in the corner of the shop as I leaned back against the brick wall and said what's up.

Tim's paternal grandfather and grandmother lived out in Seattle and had built up a fairly successful chain of specialty food stores prior to retiring and enjoying the good life. They were both hard working folks that had come over from Poland during World War II without much more than the clothes on their backs and the legal documents required for entry. They were simple people who had helped many others along the way including my friend and his family more than once. Apparently, they had been sitting at home one Sunday afternoon when a young guy that lived nearby knocked on their door. Neither one of them gave it much thought as they both knew their neighbor and had no reason to expect any type of trouble from him. It turns out they were both wrong. He said that he had a problem and wondered if he could talk to them about it. He began to explain that he was about to be evicted because he had lost his job and could not make his lease payment. Grandma went to make some tea as the old man sat and listened as their guest continued. He had supposedly had a run of bad luck, part of which was from sports betting, and as his parents were both deceased he felt that he had no one else to turn to. Grandma came back and served them both tea and some leftover coffee cake and the old man put his hand on hers as he thanked her and looked into her still sparkling blue eyes. She left the room once more and as he sat down his cup of tea the old man asked him a few questions. After a while he pretty much figured out that if they said yes this time, the next time, and the time after that were inevitable. He explained to his young guest that they now lived on a fixed income and with the medical bills that they were both beginning to incur that he simply didn't have much extra money to share. He offered to ask about with some of his many business connections and attempt to help the young man get another job. He became very agitated and said that there wasn't enough time and he was going to lose his house if they didn't give him some money. The old man said again I am sorry but we simply can't do that. If helping you find another job doesn't help you I don't know what else I can offer. You're a fucking liar the man said as he abruptly sat his tea cup and saucer on the coffee table. I know you got money hid, old people like you don't trust banks! The old man was now becoming frightened and his wife came back into the parlor to see what was the matter. The now irate neighbor stood up and looking at the old women said tell me where the money is and I won't hurt you. Just tell me where the fucking money is goddamn it! The old man stood up and told him to leave or he would call the police and the much younger man turned around and threw him to the ground and walked over to grab the now crying old women by the collar. He turned to face the injured man now desperately trying to get up and said tell me where the money is or I swear to god I'll kill your wife. There was no money to tell about and as it turned out the intruder was a man of his word. He beat the old women until she couldn't even cry anymore and when this didn't work he turned his fists and his feet on the old man.

The next day a friend that stopped by every Tuesday to have lunch, saw the two elderly people lying on the living room floor through the front window and quickly called the local police. The old man would recover but his wife of 53 years had died of head trauma from the attack. Tim and his family all flew out for the funeral and after reading the police report they were both devastated and infuriated. Later the assailant had tried to pawn some of the expensive silver service he was able to steal from the old couple. The pawn shop owner had received a BOLO describing some of the stolen goods a few days prior and stalled the man as he waited for police to arrive. When they got him to the station he lawyered up but with fingerprints and DNA they easily tied him to the crime. Once he realized he was screwed he offered up a drug use defense and as he had never been convicted of anything else the prosecutors were willing to make a deal. The murderer was already counting his lucky stars when his lawyer discovered an error in the investigation and long story got the case dismissed. No one in the family could believe it. What kind of a justice system lets a guy walk when they knew damn well he did it, had the evidence to prove it, and had a fucking confession to go along with it all. Tim was beside himself as he explained the situation to me. So, he said are you still in the business or not. I took a swig off my diet coke as I said there's three things in this world that make me want to hurt somebody, people who mess with kids, people who abuse animals, and anybody who hurts old people...I'm in.

He asked me what it would cost and I said we could discuss that later. I need some information and I'll get to work. I got a copy of the police report from Seattle PD and had my internet guy get me a bunch of stuff on the target. As it turns out, the dude's parents where both still very much alive. Their son was just so much of a loser, handout asking, low life they simply stopped having much to do with him. The son was now working again as a bartender at some chicken wings and beer brew pub and actually did have a drug habit, although nothing like he had claimed. I got into the city the next weekend and after checking in at a Motel 6 on the outskirts of town decided to head down for some wings and brew. The removal wasn't working that night but I was able to find out that one, he was working the next night, and two, most of his coworkers thought about as much of him as his parents did. I came back the next night and grabbed a seat at the bar and a menu as I began to study for the job. Terry was decent looking. Unfortunately, his arrogant personality kept any girl worth having from giving him the time of day. He asked me if I was a local or what and I explained that I was here on business. Of course he asked what kind and I said the entertainment business. He said okay as he wiped the bar and came back to check on me a few times as I ate my dinner. I knew that most restaurants post the schedules near the waiter station so as I acted like I was looking for the bathroom I ask a girl who was filling waters if she could tell me when my niece would be working again. She smiled as she looked up on the wall and asked her name. I made one up and she said she didn't see that name on the schedule. I laughed and said she's a goof ball. She goes by different nick names occasionally. If I could possibly look at the schedule I'd probably recognize one of them. The flighty girl began to tell me about a friend of hers who did something similar and she said I'm not supposed to, but I suppose it won't hurt, as she let me take a look. I went back up to the bar to pay my bill and as I handed it back Terry said peace out brother. I absolutely hate that saying, and I'm damn sure not your brother, but I smiled and said thanks as I headed out.

That night I had a current address, vehicle type and plates, and a work schedule for the next two weeks on my friend Terry. I came back in two days and again sat at the bar. After a while shithead came up and started blathering on about himself. As I listened I began to make mental preparations for how I wanted to remove him as I sipped on my beer and smiled to myself. Didn't you say you was in the entertainment business? he asked. Yes I did. What kind, like music, or movies, what? I smiled and said that I did produce a certain type of movie but you probably wouldn't see my work at the local theatre. He paused with a dumb look on his face and then his eyes brightened up as he said dude, you make porn movies! We prefer to call it adult entertainment, but yes, that is what I do. You're not some weirdo fag are you and I laughed and said no my friend. I like pussy as much as the next guy and I get plenty. Terry was now in little boy dream land. This guy has the best job in the world! I've heard that you guys shoot a lot of them around here. You rent out houses and warehouses or stuff like that. I nodded my head and said yes, sometimes. Wow, wow, he said as he went to pour the waiting servers their backed up drink orders. The next thing he did was exactly what 99% of young guys will say if you tell them you make pornos, he asked me for a job. I laughed and said man do you know how many times I get asked that? It's not as easy as you think and the one thing that true is yes, you do need a big dick. He smirked and explained that he had no problem in that department. Again, this is what most guys would probably tell you, but whatever. I said I'll tell you what, you're a decent looking guy and I can tell you stay in shape. I presented him with a business card that had a fake studio address on it. Actually it was an office that was for rent and I had asked to look at, posing as a potential tenant. While inside, I unlocked one of the windows and would return later to pull the lock, bringing it to a local lock shop the following morning, where they happily cut me a duplicate key. I told him to meet me for a screening Saturday at 11 am and he asked me what to wear. I looked at him and laughed out loud as I said do you really think we give shit. He said peace out again and my patience was really beginning to wear thin, but again I smiled as I left the bar.

Saturday was the best day as walking traffic would be minimal at an office complex. When Terry arrived I gave him a pair of sexy men's briefs I had purchased at a local XXX and told him to go in the restroom and put them on to get ready for the girls who should be here any minute. The reason I did this was to guarantee he wasn't holding a weapon when he walked out. When he did

I opted for a blunt approach as I jabbed him solidly in the solar plexus with an aluminum bat, and then cracked him on the head hard enough to knock him out but not kill him. I dressed him back in his clothes as I strapped him into the portable wheel chair I had brought along. I duct taped his mouth as I waited for darkness to fall and checked my email on my laptop. Isis gave me an update on her pregnancy and it turned out it was probably going to be twins. She sent me a picture of her little round belly with our babies inside and for a moment I felt like I was back home getting ready to watch a college football game on TV and drink a micro brew but my work was starting to wake up and it was dark enough now to go for a ride.

I had duct taped his mouth but right before we left I forced him to take two Valium as I threatened to cut his cock off if he didn't. I waited another hour for the drugs to take effect and as I pushed him towards the waiting van he was as mellow as jello and I knew I wasn't going to have any resistance as we went for our little drive into the mountains. After we were on the road for about an hour I pulled the van up onto a dirt road I had found while exploring the previous week. Washington state was a huge mining area in the day and now had literally hundreds of abandoned mine shafts that while illegal to do so, where often easy to explore. I turned the lights down to low as I made the brief five minute jaunt up the old and forgotten dusty track. At the top was a boarded up shack and a dilapidated cavern entrance which connected to a mine shaft some 50 yards in. I pulled Terry out of the van and wheeled him into the roughly constructed entryway. He was still pretty buzzed and I easily transferred him to a two-wheeled dolly I had customized slightly for the job. I put on my head lamp as I began to wheel the young assailant down the angled shaft that would take us 150 yards deep into the mountain. As we got to the second main mining cavern I wheeled Terry up to a wall that I had previously installed two eyed bolts attached to carabineers at three feet above the floor and spaced about two feet apart. As I secured him and the cart to the wall I gave him a shot of morphine to knock him out again and started to make preparations.

When he finally woke up a few hours later he would slowly start to become more coherent to his situation. Eventually he would see the small cordless circular saw and the white envelope with a letter inside. When he opened the letter it was all spelled out for him.

Hi Terry, you don't know me but I'm the one who decided if you lived or died. My employers want you to die a horrible death for what you did to that old couple but I figured I would at least give you a change to save your pathetic life. You'll notice I have placed strategically located restraints to allow you only to pick up the saw and this letter and not be able to reach any other point but the area on your right leg just below the knee.

You will also notice that I have secured a large chain and lock around the ankle on this same leg and attached it tightly to the ceiling above you. It must feel like a bad bungee jump at this point, but anyway. The situation is simple my friend, you have enough room to cut off your own leg, thus freeing yourself and with a few additional maneuvers on your part, escape dying in an abandoned mineshaft. I have already placed a tourniquet above your knee and taken the liberty of giving you a shot that will prevent you from dying of shock if you have the balls to do it. Think of it this way; I'm going to allow you the chance that you never offered your victims. You don't even deserve that but I've placed a pretty big wager that you won't, so maybe I can make some additional cash off the whole thing. By the way, you only have one hours light left in the portable halogen light above your head so I wouldn't waste time. It is currently night-time outside of the cave and you're going to have a hard enough time making it out alive as it is.

Don't let me down me friend.

As Terry took in the seriousness of his situation he knew the letter was legit as he grasped the cordless circular saw in his right hand and tried to get up the nerve to save his own life. The first cut hit him like a bolt of lightning as he screamed out loud. The second try was much like the first but numbness and shock were starting to hit and the task became a little less aggravating, but only a little. He quickly vomited twice from the pain but still he kept on, reaching upwards to cut like an animal in a trap. As his leg came free he quickly used the remaining juice in the saw to cut the restraints that were now within his reach. Free, he dropped the saw and frantically began to tighten the tourniquet as the floor began to turn black from his own blood. With the blood flow mainly stopped he began to drag himself up the long rock strewn path to survival. After 20 minutes and at about the half-way point he noticed another light up ahead. When he reached it he saw another envelope marked read. Barely able to see from exhaustion and the pain-induced sweat in his eyes he tore open the envelope and tightly gripped the white typed letter inside.

Hi again,

Sorry, but if you made it to this letter your still fucked, although I commend you on your fortitude. I really didn't think you had it in you. Just goes to show you I guess. If you reach up you can point the floodlight up the path and you will see that I've collapsed the entrance to the shaft. As he pointed the light to reveal the impenetrable rock wall he collapsed and began to scream and sob, although he had no audience. *You see my friend I had to at least have a little fun with you. It would have been far too easy to shoot you at your apartment or on the way home from work but someone like you deserves a little extra attention. I hope as you live out what will maybe be the next 10 hours, all in the darkness and alone, you feel just a little bit closer to the hell you will most certainly end up in.*

BTW;

Peace out

Twenty-Five

The Caloosahatchee River divides Ft. Myers Florida and North Ft. Myers in more than just geographical terms. Ft. Myers is known for Thomas Edison, Deon Sanders, Estero Island beach, and thousands of glazy eyed tourists slowing down the traffic in high season and taking pictures of every fucking palm tree like they'd never seen one before. The only real fun in the town was cheap liquor, great fishing, and horny tourist women. At least that's what any honest local will tell you. North Ft. Myers on the other hand is another animal all together. While only separated by a quarter mile wide river, peoplewise it's about as similar as New York City and Podunk Mississippi. While North Ft. Myers is home to a blend of working class folks, snow bird retirees, fisherman, single mothers, those trying to stay off the radar, and trailer parks, its cozy cousin on the south side of the river is where all the sophisticated people like to live. While I can enjoy the finer things of life as much as the next guy, I'm definitely more relaxed in the country. This, and the fact that you can enjoy just so many cold beers, piña coladas, and flirty 40 year-old divorcees is the reason I found myself eventually headed north one day on old U.S. 31. I needed three things; a cold glass of iced tea, some real BBQ, and time to mentally debrief myself after the cluster fuck job I had just finished.

I had the top down on the black and silver '67 SS Camaro I had rented for a couple days. The Allman Brothers *Blue Sky* blasting on the radio and a couple of joints of some of south Florida's finest tightly rolled and stashed in the glove box. I needed to clear my head and this was about the best formula I could come up with on short notice, and away from home. As I said the job I had just come off was a bit of a cluster fuck. The target was dead, so in that sense it was a success, but the job itself was pure chaos. I don't normally work with anyone else and maybe I'm a control freak but I'm also still alive and I've never been pinched. I was sub-contracting my skills as a paid favor to an associate of an associate, again something I don't typically entertain. The removal was a loud talking, horribly dressed, super sized fat motherfucker that liked to deal blow, X, and any other pills he could buy on the cheap. This prick hustled more fake shit than he did real but that was only part of the reason he had to go. Removals are never personal. If they are you have someone else do it for a number of reasons, but I have to admit that after reading the sheet on this guy and having watched and listened to him for a few weeks, I honestly wanted to say fuck the professional etiquette, and just walk up and ice pick this piece of trash in the back of the head. Crude but effective, you hit them at the base of the skull and if you know what you're doing, not only will they never so much as take another breath, there is no blood. You see the Modula Oblongata is at the base of the human skull, controls all motor function and is filled with mainly fluid as opposed to blood. So when you penetrate it with a shank, an ice pick, or any other suitable sharp pointed instrument, the target goes bye- bye like right now, and there is no mess or even any visible evidence that they just got clipped. Eventually a decent M.E. will discover the cause of death during the autopsy but by then you're already out of the state or out of the country.

If your client doesn't care if it looks like a hit your fine, unfortunately the client on this particular job was a super rich homosexual fashion designer by the name of Brent who had a few control issues and a Napoleon complex to go with it, so it had to be clean and it had to look like an accident. I don't know why he gave a shit. He wanted the dude dead. Other people wanted the dude dead and the target in question was a well known piece of shit to the highest degree. Unfortunately, the best of plans are mislaid, too many cooks wreck the stew, use whatever cliché that fits, but this job was tarnished from conception. The first problem was letting Liberace call the shots. If I needed some nice duds I might have called him. I mean that's what he does for a living and I know shit about picking out clothes, much less designing them, so I would consult someone who does. Actually that's not true, they cost too much and are way to girly for my taste, but you get the point. Now here we have a situation where a bad guy needs to go away, the client has been referred by people who know this business very well to not one, not two, but three of the most competent killers in all of North America and yet, this sequin wearing Nancy boy wants to say what's what. This fucker actually wanted us to give him a daily report like we were a bunch of office managers or something. That was the first thing I said no to. Second, and I don't know why and don't want to know why, he wanted us to save all of the pictures and audio surveillance for later use. I think he was just some whacked out sexual freak that had let money go to his head, but again the answer was no. He protested a little and I quickly told him that if he was unhappy with my services I would encourage him to pursue other operators. The other contractors could do what they wanted, I really didn't care. This was a nice way of saying shut your hole or I walk. Anyway, back to the target.

Chip "Slick Chip" Walker represented nine out of about ten things I hate in humans. It wasn't just the dope dealing, I could give a shit how somebody else makes their living, but slick Chip was just a slimy, greedy grease ball that polluted the earth from the time he woke up until the time he went to bed. He would cheat his own grandmother out of her social security check if he could get away with it, and that was if he was having a good day. He ran scams of every variety, he owned a couple of payday advance companies that prayed on the destitute and just plain stupid. He ran an underground food stamp trade for twenty cents on the dollar to the local junkies, and only ten if it was past the 15th of the month, and of course he ran dope, but all of these could have been given a pass except for one fatal mistake on old Slick's part; he decided to get into the kiddy porn business.

Turns out it wasn't his flavor, he was just in it for the cash and there was apparently a lot of it. I guess it just goes to show you that the world still has its share of sick bastards no matter where you go. I didn't really get it. I mean although the guy lived a life that I personally wouldn't want he was making a lot of cash. Why would he even consider dirtying his clothes with something as fucked up and evil as kiddy porn? Greed; I've seen more people mess their lives up over simple greed, but again that's their choice.

Apparently one of the main ways that they get the kids that they need is buy renting them from whacked out dope addict moms or dads and in some cases baby sitters who bring the kid in to the studio, unbeknownst to anybody else. They will sometimes drug the kids or use various tactics to cajole or scare them into their deprived requests and would then do what they do. Well, one particular crack whore that slick had his noose around and had instructed to find him some models just happened to be a baby sitter for some pretty wealthy local families.

When Renee LeClair got the call from the Lee county sheriff's department that her baby sitter had been arrested with her only child and a bag of crack cocaine, she quickly swallowed a valium and a her blood pressure medication and drove as quickly as she could to the police station. Upon arrival and after hearing the current revelations in the case the pills seemed to lose their effects. She felt like she was going to lose her mind. She wanted to scream, and she wanted to throw up, and she wanted to beat the living shit out of the baby sitter who was lucky to be locked up and out of her reach, for now. She swore without any uncertainty that this bitch was going to pay, and pay dearly, and that was just a start. The detectives told her that although they already ascertained that some sexual activity had been perpetrated they didn't have all the details just yet. Part of the problem was that they had to interview traumatized children who were already slipping into various stages of mental shock and a post traumatic stress syndrome of sorts. It would take months or years of counseling and therapy to reveal their words and no one had the time to wait. The main info would have to come from the crack whore who was starting to come down off her high, which led them to question how much of her info was legit. Was it the dope talking or the hunger for more? Every addict will try and get dope from you if they're in an interview room and withdrawing. They think they hold the cards and although that may be true for a little while, the real truth is it's only a matter of time before they start shitting themselves and going into an episode of violent vomiting from the withdrawals that are certain to come. They know it and any decent investigator knows it. So who holds the cards now asshole?

We don't need all the details of what was revealed but let's just say that Renee LeClair was given more than enough motivation, and in my opinion justification, to dust some people off. She had plenty of money to pay for services and just happened to have a gay designer friend who had in the past liked to brag about his associations with the criminal underworld. Many a summer afternoon they had sat on her patio drinking hundred dollar a bottle French wine, snorting pure flake, and having girl talk over the latest fashions and finance. I don't know if he was trying to show his masculine side, the coke was doing the talking, or he was just trying to play wise guy, but Brent always had to inject some fable about his friends into their conversations, what they did to people who owed them money, how much power they had, and how tight they were with Bret. Let me just say right now that although everybody associated with my profession in any capacity considers all money as green regardless of the source, not many of them hang out with sword swallowers or consider them as paisan. Even if they did, they sure as hell wouldn't continue that affection if they heard that someone was bragging about the relationship. That's just plain stupid. I'm not being homophobic, just keeping it real. When Renee got home the first person she called was Brent.

The conversation didn't even start with small talk. She told him she needed to talk to the friends he had mentioned in the past and she needed talk to them ASAP. Brent kind of stammered and back peddled but she wasn't hearing it; time to put up or shut up big boy. She told him she would explain more in person for obvious reasons but that he better get his ass and his iphone in gear. As soon as her husband got home and took over watching their child she headed to Brent's place. What she didn't know was that although Brent knew some people, who knew some people, kind of, he himself knew no one. It was all drug-and booze-induced big talk, and now he would have to find a way to come good on his story telling. He told her to calm down, talk to no one, not even her husband, and give him a week. She said flatly you have two days. This woman was not fucking around and she made it clear. Someone had traumatized her only child and any fool knows there are some things in this world that you just don't do, and this was one of them. Brent was a nervous wreck. He felt like an anxiety ridden school boy that had just been caught with his first box of smokes and a pack of rubbers. What the fuck was he going to do? He really didn't know anybody, or at least not anybody like he had bragged about. Then he thought of his cousin Charlie in Atlanta.

He had to call his Aunt to get the number and she peppered him with questions about how his mother was, when was the last time he had talked to her, how was the clothing business, of which he reminded her that he was a designer, not a salesman, but things were good. Now please, can I have Charlie's number, he pleaded. Charlie answered on the second ring and mid way through the conversation abruptly stopped Brent to ask if he had a pen. He did and Charlie quickly gave him a number for a throw away cell phone number to write down. He said leave your house and call that number in one hour and not from your own cell or house phone, go buy a prepaid and then we'll talk. In one hour the phone rang and the conversation continued. Brent told him what had happened except he left out the part about all the shit he had talked in the past. Charlie it turns out was connected, which Brent had always suspected, hated anybody who fucked with kids, and in spite of his sexual preference and the fact that they hadn't talked in years, still had love for his cousin. They were family, what are you going to do.

Charlie told Brent first off, calm dawn, and please keep your mouth shut. It can be handled and I know people who can handle it, but patience and planning are my strong suit and not yours, so please chill the fuck out. Brent didn't feel chilled out but he knew to listen to his cousin and just said okay. Charlie explained to him that he would call tomorrow at noon and we'll then talk again from the same numbers we did today. Brent said but what about Renee to which Charlie replied, she's your problem Brent, handle your problem.

Brent got home and called Renee. She started right off with her ball buster approach and Brent, listening to his cousin's advice, finally manned up for once in his life and told her to shut the fuck up and listen for a change. It was being handled and it would be handled but it would take a minute, hypothetically speaking. She started to try and take the upper hand again and Brent, freaked out enough already by the past few days said look, if you want me to help you I will, but we do it my way and not yours because quite honestly, you don't have a way, and that's why you called me in the first place, right? Renee instantly deflated. He was right, she had money but in reality he was her only option. She had never known the kind of people who even walked in these circles, much less worked in them and she knew that right this second all she had was Brent. Other than a brief thought of driving her brand new Lincoln MKX into the projects to look for a $300 a job amateur who would probably just end up robbing her, maybe raping her, and most certainly taking her car in the process, she had no other choices.

Charlie, true to his word and reputation, set things up. One of his associates knew one of my associates and so I came to be involved. The other two operators were contracted through someone else and none of it was any of my concern. If they knew the job and were professionals I didn't give a damn about the details. Vince was from the east coast and Red was from somewhere around Seattle. Vince was the gun and car guy, Red was the bomb and chemical guy, that's all I knew and all I wanted to know and only in case I had to hunt them in the future. In this business shit happens, there is no honor system and there are no boy scouts. If one of these guys fucked up or rolled over and wanted to give the cops a gift, they needed to know that they could, and would, be found. I couldn't really figure why the job needed three of us. In my opinion Brent just had too much money and too big of an ego. This was his one chance in life to play the part of the bad ass so like many people he went for over kill, whatever.

Vince, Red, and I made camp at a pay by the week hotel in a rundown part of Ft. Myers. It wasn't my typical accommodations, but this was not my typical situation and it kept the job within the parameters of my professional motto; fly low and fly level. Being flashy will get you caught or killed and I enjoyed my freedom and my life way too much to let any uncontrolled variable allow either of these things to happen. We did our basic recon, spent some time on the internet, in local bars and restaurants, casually gleaning any information that could help us establish who the target really was and what his habits, tastes, or weaknesses were. He lived in a gated community on Sanibel Island but didn't spend a lot of time there. He had a 20-something wife with a tit job, a coke habit, and a taste for young pool boys and gardeners. They had no kids, and that was a plus in more ways than one. He spent most of his time around town dropping off product or monitoring the business end of his sleazy operations. He and his wife ate out a lot in the evenings. They pretty much never ate dinner at home. Most of the places they went to weren't really what I would consider fine dining but more of a place to be seen at and pay ridiculous prices for over dressed, gourmet food. While slick's wife was high speed and extravagant, slick was slow speed and cheap. The only time he would spent any cash was when he needed to get his wife to shut up. Wifey liked the coke but Slick liked the downers, opium, oxy, valium, ludes, Vicodin, and of course weed. After following and running surveillance on him for a couple of weeks we finally figured out our angle to hit him.

Our target, like most people, lived a life based on habits and routines. He typically woke up just before noon, went to the kitchen and made a latte or a Bloody Mary, cruised the internet, checked his email, etc. The other thing he did everyday was, at some point after he woke up, to stroll his fat ass on out to the gazebo off the main room. Slick's gazebo housed the best Jacuzzi money could buy. This thing was tricked out with every option imaginable, flat screen TV on the wall, sound system, essential oil bubbler, more jets than the air force, pillows, cup holders, the works. It also had an access panel for maintenance. Old slick would come down one day, sit back, soak up, and not have a care in the world, for the last time. In the early morning hours the day of the hit, Red, because he was the smallest and a wiring expert, snuck into the gazebo, placing a small slit in the most visibly worn part of the main water line that ran above the circuit board. Then he moved to the GFI switch that every Jacuzzi has and using a tiny portable soldering gun and a piece of uncoated lead wire, reconnected the hot and cold wires that the GFI was intended to bypass in the case of a short in the system. When the slickster got into the hot tub in the morning as he always did and switched on the jets, water would soon leak from the razor cut in the line, down onto the hot board, and because the GFI had been deactivated, fry his ass like a big old Cajun turkey at Thanksgiving. Red set it up so that the power from the short would, within minutes melt the temporary solder on the GFI and anyone inspecting it would just see it as a fluke or an undetectable defect in the system that had created a tragic accident. His widow would initiate a lawsuit and probably settle out of court, never have to marry another rich, fat guy, and spent the rest of her days screwing pool boys and service workers, with a pile of cash in the bank and a sweet ass house.

There was only one problem. On the day of the job fat boy got an unexpected call from the studio that a water line had busted in the ceiling and they had one hell of a mess on their hands, and no production for the day. Irate as hell he flew out of the house and down to the studio to chew somebody's ass. This was costing him a chunk of cash and somebody was going to pay. Twenty minutes after he left the pool boy showed up as he usually did on Tuesdays. The wife, knowing that hubby was out of the picture for at least a while told the lucky pool boy that if he could find the time she would like him to join her in the hot tub, and what guy is going to turn down an offer like that. The pool boy was just about to blow his nut when the lights went out on both of them. The wire did melt as planned but the melted lead wire Red had installed then dripped onto another connection below it somehow also shorted out and caught the cedar wood of the tub frame on fire. Within ten minutes the gardener noticed the smoke and went to investigate, about the same time slick pulled into the driveway. As the gardener began to open the door a propane tank that had been left inside of the gazebo as back up for the outside gas grill had gotten hot enough from the fire and exploded, catching the gardeners clothing on fire and sending him screaming across the back yard, yelling help me, help me in Spanish, and finally rolling like a mad man on the lawn in an attempt to put out the flames. Just then slick stepped onto the back patio. Seeing the gazebo on fire, he waddled over to see what the hell was going on and wondered out loud "what the fuck is that spic gardener doing, rolling on the lawn?" The propane tank had quickly run out of gas and he was able to walk in. Bobbing in the hot tub were the slightly charred, naked bodies of his wife and the pool boy, dead as door knobs. The site of this combined with the rolling and smoldering gardener and slick's debaucherous lifestyle, caused him to have a massive heart attack right on the spot. When the fireman showed up they quickly extinguished the fire, tended to the gardener, and called the police. It was determined the tragic accidental death of the two lovers was caused by a water leak and an electrical malfunction. The husband, they determined had died of natural causes, exacerbated by an existing heart condition.

It didn't go down the way we had planned and I never like excess casualties, but other than the pool boy no one died who probably didn't have it coming, and the gardener would heal and collect a nice chunk of cash from the insurance company, so in that respect it was kind of a success. Brent was very impressed. The dumb bastard actually thought that it was all an intricate plan that had worked without flaw. I let him believe it, and upped the fee accordingly. He was a fucking chatterbox and I think being around people who killed people made him really nervous. He tried not to show it, but it's my experience that when somebody simply won't shut the fuck up they're probably nervous as a whore in church, and designer boy was no exception. I swear I thought he was going to ask me for a business card when I finally had enough of listening to him and said "Brent, you owe me ninety grand, and I'd like my money sometime before the end of the year," and I wasn't smiling. He got the point and quickly produced the cash in a small briefcase which I counted without looking at him any further. As he rambled on thanking me and giving me the typical "if your ever in Florida again bullshit," as I was headed out the door. What a douche bag.

Six months later Brent, while driving home on a beautiful Florida evening tuned up on Vicodin and chardonnay, crossed the center line and ran head on into a semi-truck filled with his own line of designer clothing, killing him instantly. I guess life sometimes has a very strange sense of humor...

Twenty-Six

As I headed north on old 41 I looked forward to seeing the swamp boys again. I had met George and Scott Black while on another job up in Sarasota some years ago. I ran into George at a local oyster bar sucking down fresh steamed shell fish and washing it all down with ice cold Coronas at the bar. George was a good old boy but had spent his early years growing up in New York so he had some city boy flair left in him. He was one hell of a dancer and had the gift of gab which proved to his favor with the ample supply of sun kissed beauties in Florida. I remember the first night I met him he was trying to get with this girl from Bradenton when her boyfriend and a few of his redneck buddies showed up. George only ran about 5' 11" but his frame was packed with muscle from the life he had lived and a brief period of power lifting a few years back. It was started to get pretty heated for my new buddy and I wasn't sure if I was going to get involved. I assumed he could handle himself but when two more dip chewing hillbillies joined the four already primed to whoop his ass I couldn't just sit by. Just as George and I were ready to square off his brother Scotty showed up with a big old grin and asked the boyfriend what the problem was.

The dude said that George was trying to screw his girlfriend and Scott kind of laughed as he placed his hand on the other guys shoulder and said can you blame him? I mean look at the tits on that gal. If I though Scott was going to calm things down I couldn't have been more wrong and he hauled off and cold cocked the now very pissed off boyfriend. Everything from there on was about 20 minutes of chaos, breaking bottles, and fists flying. In the end we bolted just before the cops showed up with our shirts torn to shit and the two brothers laughing hysterically while rating our success in the brawl, jokingly trying to one up each other as we drove to another more civilized drinking establishment. By the end of the night I was pretty drunk and my car was back at the other bar, so they insisted I crash at their house and they would help me get my car in the morning. I took them up on their generous offer and woke up the next day with two damn good friends to have.

As I pulled into the long drive I saw the ample supply of No Trespassing signs they had bordering the entrance and they weren't kidding even a little. Their daddy had left them this place and it was all of around 500 acres of mixed hardwoods and cypress with two really good fishing streams running right through the middle of it, and a huge swamp bordering the rear of the property that, if you knew where you were going ended up emptying into the nearby Gulf of Mexico. They raised pit bulls for hunting feral pigs and were quite handy with catching gators and snakes, as well. They made a decent living off trapping and skinning and would occasionally get hired by one of the local cities to capture a gator or a big critter that was causing a problem, and was so far avoiding capture by the hired guns. The abundant swamps had lots of alligators and cottonmouths but with the rapid development of south Florida the local wildlife was beginning to venture into areas that were made for city folks and not animals. They would get calls for everything from black bears and puma's, to the occasional mountain lion, which many believed didn't exist until they brought one back spitting mad in a cage in the back of their Ford pickup truck. I had enjoyed many a meal and a cold glass of iced tea on the front porch and as I pulled up to the house George Jr. walked out carrying a double barrel 12 gauge coach gun that was damn near bigger than he was. As I got out I looked directly at him as I pulled off my sunglasses and said son put that thing down before it goes off on you and somebody gets hurt. He smiled wide as he replied mister, if this gun goes off it will be hitting exactly who I intended it to; that I'll guarantee you. He set the gun down as he ran up to give me a bear hug and I said son you are sure as hell a chip off the old block as we walked into the log cabin to see everybody else.

The girls were cooking a lunch of fried mackerel the boys had caught that morning along with some stewed okra and tomatoes, and a hot pan of corn bread fresh out of the oven. I could hear the dogs barking as the rest of the crew showed up and after a round of more hugs and back slapping, we all sat down to eat. We talked a little about life up north and down here. We all griped about politicians, agreeing the biggest crooks were still in Washington and always would be as we changed the subject to something more fun like fishing, drinking, and chasing our wives. I told them that Isis was pregnant and most likely with twins. The wives made me promise to bring them all down after the babies were born and I did. After a while Scott said they had some work to finish and wondered if I wanted to go for a swamp boat ride. I was both excited at the thought of hauling ass through the back country and seeing my friends after such a long spell, as I said I'll grab the cooler! We loaded up the truck and headed off to the dock with the airboat a short ten minute ride away. When we got there I checked out fuel and topped off the tanks as they both made a mental checklist of all the other items you always carried for survival in one of the most unforgiving places in America. With the cooler, two AR-15 rifles with lots of back up clips, and a few other items, we headed off to the hunting shack in the middle of the thick marshland. As we approached I could see the chimney lightly spewing smoke and I guessed they had been here earlier in the day. We tied up the boat and as we walked into the room I could see what they needed to finish.

He looked like he was Cuban or maybe Puerto Rican. Whatever he was this wasn't his finest hour and I could see the scorpion bites starting to swell on his hands and feet. George and Scott were great guys and regular church going family men. They also had some other natural abilities that allowed them to become very good at another type of side work. They had both been taught by their dad and his brothers pretty much everything there was to know about surviving in a swamp. They could hunt, fish, skin, trap, and live off the local plants and wildlife without ever needing to see civilization another day in their lives. As Scott once said the only down side is the girls hate the swamp so we have to come out here when we can. The guy in the chair was looking a mixture of pissed off and ready to crap his pants. The bites on his hands and feet where from a bug-box that the boys invented a few years back. It was made of Plexiglas and had a hole cut in the top with a neoprene fitting that had several slits cut into it. They could load it with scorpions or spiders and would then force either the hand or the bare foot of their target into the hole. The bugs could have as much fun as they needed but when you pulled the hand or foot back out, the neoprene scraped them right back into the safe confines of the box, with the unwilling participant screaming through the gag in his mouth. They had given this guy three times already but he said he wouldn't talk so they had left to go have lunch. It was now time for plan B and they brought out the snake bag. I could see the Cuban guy's eyes nervously watching the very active cloth receptacle. He didn't have a clue what was in it but I'm sure his imagination was running wild right about now. They explained to him that the cottonmouth they had caught and kept in the bag was now both very angry and eagerly waiting to bite anything that happened to get stuck inside the bag with it. Scotty looked at him and said maybe it's your arm, or maybe your manhood, we haven't quite decided yet. I could see him start to sweat and George got pissed off and said "amigo we're done fuckin' around with you." I got fish to catch and beer to drink with my friend here, as he pointed in my direction. If this don't work I'm just gonna throw your ass to my pet gator outside and I'll tell the folks in Miami that you wouldn't talk, and I'll only get half my pay. Either way, I'm thirsty and I haven't seen my bro here in a while, so it's your call. They ripped off the gag and old boy started talking and wouldn't shut up. They had a MP3 digital recorder that they could transfer to email and after 15 minutes they had what they wanted and shot the guy in the back of the head with a short rifle 22 round. It makes less noise and you don't have to worry about it coming out. Actually, its one of my weapons of choice for the pop and drop jobs that occasionally come along. They dumped him in the swamp on the ride back and the alligators would have their meal after all, but at least he wouldn't feel it.

When we got back to the house the girls who knew I loved barbeque had gone all out. They drove into town to get some brisket, pulled pork, and chicken. When they got back they went to fixing homemade hush puppies, coleslaw, dirty rice, and mixed greens with side pork from their own freezer. Big jars of tea and lemonade were on the table along with two huge baskets of bis-cuits and an old metal Coca Cola cooler like they used to have at the drive-in theaters were sitting on the ground packed full of Bud Lite and Corona. After we cleaned up we sat down with the whole family and a few cousins who came buy as we ate, drank, laughed, and danced to Cajun and country music until the early morning hours of the next day.

Twenty-Seven

At first I couldn't understand the frail male voice on the other end of the line. I knew from the caller ID that it was a call from Sicily and I assumed it was dad but this didn't sound like him. The voice on the other end was a man collapsing within himself, the words weak and trembling. This could not be our father, our father was strong, confident, and full of passion. I didn't know who the stranger on the other end was but in the weeks that followed I would.

As his words became clearer I would come to realize that our adoptive mother and his wife of almost 60 years had died in her sleep the night before. We had told them that my wife was pregnant, and now the only thing I could think of was how she would never see her grandchildren or hold them while they cuddled the stuffed animals she had given me in anticipation of their coming into the world. I was thankful that she hadn't suffered but at the same time I was sick to my stomach over my concern for my dad. He never even got a chance to say goodbye. He told me that just before she went to sleep she kissed him while he sat reading as she always did right before bed. I hoped that this would help him a little but I couldn't begin to comprehend losing someone that you had loved that long. I met Diamo in Palermo and we helped father plan the funeral and tried to do whatever we could to ease his pain which just wasn't possible. For as strong and viral of a man as Armando Bruno was, the breath in his lungs and the sparkle in his eyes was now laying cold in a morticians prep room somewhere in town. We had the funeral at the villa. We knew she would have wanted it that way and in our country this was much more accepted than having your loved ones last hours above ground spent in some funeral parlor. The neighbor ladies kept busy preparing food and coffee as the men, all dressed in black, congregated in the sitting room. When it came time for the priest to speak he talked briefly about eternal life and how important our faith in God was particularly during times of grief. He said that our mother had gone now to her heavenly father, but for me that didn't help ease my pain at all. I didn't want her in heaven. I wanted her here stroking my father's hand, singing in the kitchen, and asking my wife questions about what color she was going to paint the nursery. Diamo stayed by our father and didn't say a lot. I guessed this was his way of handling it and I respected his privacy.

They carried her in a horse drawn carriage adorned with a thousand roses as the people along the road came out to pay their respects. We all followed in black limousines and when we reached the gravesite father got out and could barely support himself as my brother and I each took him gently by an arm and guided him to a chair by the grave. The wind blew slightly as the priest said a few more words. Mother had insisted on being buried next to Angelia and the pain of her choice, combined with the beauty of her love, made it a surreal moment for me. It was a beautiful sunny day and I couldn't help but think that if she was going to be laid to rest, there was no better day for it and no better place.

We stayed in country for three more weeks mainly spending our time sitting with our father and going for rides back out to the cemetery. He wasn't eating much but seemed to be gaining back some of his strength, as he insisted on tending her plot. Some days we would just let him sit by her grave and from a distance I could see his lips moving as he gently talked her and stroked the rose quartz head stone with his pale and aging hands. Finally one day he told us it was time to go home. We were both torn as we did not want to abandon the man who had done so much for us. He asked me if I remembered his words when Angelia had died and I told him I had. Well now Dominick it is I who must heed my own advice. Your mother and I had a long time together and lived a very blessed life but now she has gone and I am left to carry on as you were when Angelia died. I sat awe struck at his courage as I paused for consideration of the fact that I had lost my first love when I was only a teenager with my entire life in front of me. Armando had just buried the women he had spent most of his life with and was now almost

80 with only so many spring days left to greet him. We respected his wishes and flew back to our respective cities a few days later. On the flight back I found myself challenging some of my own personal beliefs and asking internal and quite intimate questions that would plague me for many months to come.

Even before this all happened I was beginning to ponder my work. I had been doing removals now for over 20 years, and I can say without exception that I had not one regret about anyone I had taken out. Still something was lingering in my subconscious and until I figured out what it was I had decided to take a hiatus. My wife was getting further along in her pregnancy and although her checkups had all been as they should be, I found myself in a constant state of concern for her and our unborn children. I would wake up in the middle of the night many times a week and just sit in the darkness as I watched her breath, worrying in my head sometimes that at any moment it might just stop. I think most of it was from the cancer scare with my brother followed by our mother passing. I don't care who you are, losing people you love makes you consider your own mortality, and if you have a pregnant wife when it happens you can't help but become overly aware of the very fragile nature of life. I went to the appointments with her and that helped to calm my nerves. I spent a lot of time reading and most of it was stuff I never would have given a second thought five years ago. I always loved adventure stories and crime drama, but now found myself picking books about spiritual awareness, psychology, and even some philosophy off the library shelves. My change of reading interest is what would eventually give me the answer to the question that had been bothering me.

Twenty-Eight

I was beginning to enjoy my work, and this was my problem. For most people this would be a blessing and something that many could aspire to and never quite reach. For me however it was a character flaw, and one that I myself had created. When I first started out it had always been just business but somewhere along the way, and I honestly can't say when, I began to take it on a more personal level. I began to realize that my rules were my insulation from having to look in the mirror at a sociopath. I possessed the off switch that 98% of the world did not. I could stalk my target for weeks, end them in a matter of minutes, and be enjoying a good meal or a night out a short time later with absolutely no afterthoughts. When I killed I simply cleaned up my work and put everything back in order much like a woodworker does after building a bench. Whatever happened later was my personal time with no consideration of the day's duties. It was like I was a factory worker punching out at the end of a shift at the time clock and then meeting my buddies for a beer later. It was no different. How in the hell had I come to now enjoying something that my instincts had always told me I shouldn't?

It wasn't like I could hire a shrink or attend some form of group therapy; hi, my name is Dominick and I'm a contract killer, and the group would respond; hi Dominick!! This wasn't AA and that wasn't going to happen. So then what? Why all of a sudden did I get a conscience about my work? Nothing had changed with the business. The world still had plenty of people in it who needed to die. Nothing had changed, so why was I? I had to put my new religion on hold for a moment as, like it or not, I still had a job to perform. I was heading back to Chicago for a week to straighten out some mob and gang conflict over territory and if ever there was a time that I needed a clear head it was now. Apparently some of the local street muscle had grown overly confident and where attempting to move in on turf that had long been controlled by the local Italian boys. There had been insults made and couriers killed and this wasn't something that a sit down would fix. Tony "The Diamond Don" Scalisi had been running the upper West side just as his father had, and his father before him. He got the nickname from his preference for jewel heists as a young wise guy and in later years because of his flashy appearance. He dressed in handmade suits and always wore charcoal black, silver, or shark skin. He bought nothing but the finest Italian leather shoes and had a collection of watches that would make most rappers envious. He really was a class act but he was also someone you did not play around with, not if you knew what was good for you. He had always enjoyed a professional understanding with the other families and in recent years had even worked amicably with the local black and Latino organized crime groups as well. Most of his money was made the old fashioned way with underground gambling, loan sharking, protection money, and of course the girls. He had some legitimate businesses but most of it was just for show or to wash money from the other operations. They made a small amount off the local drug trade but mainly as a whole sale supplier and not so much in a retail capacity. He earned some juice but there was always plenty of profit margin left for the people in the down line. Tony was smart, not greedy, and the whole thing could have been a long lasting and easy payday for everyone involved, but as usual a couple of people decided they wanted more, and those same people began to let their mouth write a check that their ass could not cover...

The two main street gangs in this part of town were the West Side Locos and the Uptown Hustlers. Both operated much like corporations and were highly structured in their business affairs. In my experience most gangs are more efficient and disciplined than many fortune 500 CEO's you read about but one day somebody decided that they wanted to expand, and then somebody else, seeing them making moves, decided that maybe they wanted more too. Before you know it pride and money lust had overtaken common sense and long term thinking and although the gangs were very impressive in some areas, the Italian mafia had been very efficient at handling problems well before any of the local street groups had rented their first clubhouse. As I understood it the don had actually invited the two gang leaders to his office to try and come to an understanding. He had treated them with respect and, being schooled in proper business etiquette, had made every reasonable attempt to rectify the current situation at a management level. Unfortunately, he didn't receive the same in return. The gangs had guns and they had plenty of soldiers. They basically told him that things were changing and he could either get used to it or he could go fuck himself. Neither one of them cared very much which option he chose. Tony offered his apologies that things could not be settled and shaking both of their hands wished them well in the future. After they had left he and his captains sat back and sipped espresso as they considered the whole situation. When it was decided that diplomacy was no longer an option once again I received a phone call.

The country of Italy has never really been known for its military success. Historically the soldiers always preferred to eat, drink wine, and chase women, as opposed to fight. La Cosa Nostra on the other hand had born leaders from its inception that were well schooled in the strategy of war. Among their most popular influences was Niccolo Machiavelli, a 14th century Italian writer, and at one time a government official. His basic philosophy was simple; if you have to fight don't screw around. Go hardcore or don't even start. He had some finesses moves but when it came time to fight there weren't any rules. The Italian military may not have taken his wisdom to heart but the mafia sure did. When I met with Tony he explained his predicament in detail. He wasn't making that much off the drug trade, and truth be told he had been making legitimate business investments for years that would soon allow him to exit the trade altogether. The problem was he simply couldn't let these thugs walk around disrespecting his position. If you let one get away with it, before you knew it everyone else was. Soon your street respect was gone and your business interests wouldn't be far behind. As we discussed the situation I inquired how he preferred it be handled. I wasn't sure if he just wanted the two mouths taken out or their whole crew. He explained that with having two enemies the tactics changed. If you had only one problem you hit them hard and fast and in public if possible, to sent a message to the streets. With two there came other elements of attack and considerations to be had. You had to be aware of retaliation and collateral damage. While not prohibitive in nature, a wise man gave them a high degree of respect. Tony said that in his opinion the best way to solve the problem was not to go head to head with them, but to make the two of them fight each other. Why waste your soldiers when you could make them waste theirs.

The Locos had a place on east 74th street that they liked to sit in front of drinking Mexican beer and showing off their tattoos to the chicas strolling the street. Pussy, money, and power, that's all anybody was interested in and they spent most of their waking hours pursuing one or the other. What they weren't really good at was noticing vehicles parked on the street that did not belong there. I had bought a beat up white panel van with dark tinted windows, a privacy wall between the front and the back, and a hole in the side that allowed me to sit for hours as I watched and listened to the conversation. The uptown hustlers had a similar situation but at least they had lookouts posted on the roof. After only a week, and with input from the Don, I formulated a very simple plan. I rented an apartment on the fourth floor of a building across the alley behind the clubhouse. From my vantage point I could easily view both the front and rear exits along with any rooftop activity. After only a couple days I had figured out the schedule for the lookouts, who was paying attention, and who was on their cell phone most of the time. One guy always carried a pint of tequila in his vest and half way through the night watch would have both a good buzz and an empty bottle. I'd had some difficult jobs before but this wasn't going to be one of them. It was a warm Tuesday night and I had parked the white van kitty-corner from the Loco's club house. I watched them smoke a few joints, sipping on beer, and enjoying the Latino girls without a care in the world. I had a Mac-10 with silencer and 30 round clips sitting next to me. I would have preferred an Uzi or even a Heckler and Koch MP-5 for both firepower and efficiency, but Mac-10's were what the gangs used and I was going to leave this one behind for the survivors to find. I stepped out of the van into the darkness with gloved hands, sunglasses, a blue dew rag, and the small submachine gun wrapped in a dark cloth hanging at my side. I easily got within 20 feet of them and as the first guy noticed me I opened up with a three round burst to his chest. They all started scrambling and reaching for their guns, but between the dope and the beer I had a clear advantage as I killed seven of them before dropping my first clip. I ran into the main door and sprayed the place, killing a few more and wounding several. They were lucky I wasn't just some random shooter and actually knew how to handle a weapon, otherwise their girlfriends would have been among the victims. I visually swept the place for threats. Finding none I walked back outside and confirmed I had iced the main guy I wanted to, the one that told Tony to go fuck himself. I dropped the gun and my dew rag as I headed off in the van to start phase two.

The hustlers had on-street parking in front of their place. When I pulled up a few of them gave me a look but nothing else as I grabbed some empty pizza boxes out of the rear for a fake delivery and disappeared around the corner. I had constructed a Salerno's Pizza sign that was attached to the side of the van facing the hangout and would come in real handy in a matter of hours. I got up to the apartment and watched my tequila drinking friend for a while as I readied myself. At quarter after midnight I was listening to the cell scanner and I picked up a conversation where someone said the Loco's had been hit and were already talking about hitting back. No one in the Hustler's clubhouse new anything about an attack on the other club but that didn't prevent them from becoming very agitated and visibly on guard. It was show time and I went over to the now open fourth floor window, making sure the guards were preoccupied, and very carefully lobbed the three pound satchel of explosives where they came to rest right by the rear entrance of the clubhouse. In exactly five minutes the timer went off as a big fire ball shot 20 feet in the air and the whole building shook. The rooftop look outs hit the deck but just as I assumed got up and ran towards the back of the building to see what the hell had just happened. With the CAR-15 I easily put a kill shot in both of their heads, sprayed the rear door with a full clip, and waited for the bees to come out of the hive. I had deliberately placed my first explosion at the rear of the building knowing that the occupants would assume they were being attacked from the blind side. Bangers don't have the skills or the training to face a full on assault toe-to-toe, so out the front door they all began to run. It was a group of around ten guys and some had pistols and shotguns out as they looked around to see if anyone was shooting at the front. They were standing right in front of the pizza delivery van when explosion number two went off.

It really was just a matter of psychology and tactical training. I had built the fake sign with a dozen homemade claymore mines imbedded in it at strategic points. I had used double aught buckshot pellets and just enough powder to cause the lethal projectiles to completely saturate the immediate area in front of the sign but not enough to do any further damage to surrounding buildings or people. In a matter of seconds the primary leadership of the uptown hustlers was either dead or dying on the dirty sidewalk. I had placed some dynamite in a box by the fuel tank and remote detonated it to shred the van and limit the evidence gathering ability of the Chicago PD, not that they really gave a damn. For most this was just a case of a few more assholes shooting each other over drug turf. As long as there weren't civilian casualties the investigation would be perfunctory as best. The next few months were spent by the remaining gang members continually attempting to avenge their brothers. The last thing on anyone's mind was the Italians and pretty soon they had decimated each other's ranks to a degree where other local groups easily moved in and took over their drug corners, but none of them ever thought about fucking with The Diamond Don again. Tony had a lot of local cops and even some feds on his payroll. When I came to collect my fee he said that he had some information that I needed to hear. I assumed it was for a future job which I really wanted to decline but he said calmly, Dominick, you have a problem...

What now I thought, as I grabbed a crystal glass of ice and scotch and found a seat in a tall leather backed chair. Tony began to explain that he had friends in the FBI. In the last week my name had come up as a possible suspect in the abduction of those dirt bags from St. Louis. Nobody really cared that much about that part of the deal. The problem I had was twofold; one of the guards I gassed that night had a heart problem and the damn gas, combined with the stress of the whole thing had killed him. It might have stopped at a state level but son of a bitch if he wasn't actually a federal prison guard who had taken a shift doing the county prisoner transport for some extra pay. What should have been a minimal state corrections affair had become a full blown FBI investigation. This wasn't good, this was not good at all, but then I remembered how clean the whole job had gone and was sure they could never find the farm or the remains of the bodies. As it turned out I was right unfortunately, that kid I had let live remembered my face and my tattoo.

———————————————

Twenty-Nine

What do I do? How much do the feds know, and how close are they? All of these were questions that I could not share with my wife and I was scared. I wasn't so concerned with actually going to prison. With ability comes options, and I automatically began to consider every one of them but I now had a wife with two kids on the way and that changed things. If it was just me I would have disappeared the next week. I had plenty of cash and could liquidate my investments and portfolio in a matter of days with only a minimal loss for doing it. If I needed to I could leave the U.S. with just over $1.4 million and with that much cash I would make a new life, with a new identity, in a country that did not have an extradition agreement with this one, but again I had a wife. Tony assured me that he would get weekly updates from his informant and I would know if and when they were coming for me, well before it actually happened. I appreciated this resource but it did little to make me stop thinking about the whole thing. I could not believe that because of one of the only times in my life I showed some fucker mercy, my whole world was coming undone. I wondered if my dad would have let the guy live. Hopefully I would still be able to ask him that question someday. I decided not to tell my wife just yet. There wasn't any point and if it caused her to miscarriage I would never forgive myself. I was pretty sure she didn't know the other side of my business and I wanted it to stay that way as long as possible.

I spent more time at home and started working out at a local gym to keep myself active. I had put all jobs on hold as I didn't know if I was being watched and sure as hell didn't need them getting any more information on other hits. I quickly and quietly sold off a few properties, transferring all of the proceeds into cashier's and travelers checks in my wife's name drawn on an international bank and kept in a safe deposit box. Occasionally, Tony would call and give me an update. I had never been arrested or had my fingerprints taken so the national database wasn't going to help them. I wasn't on any of the Interpol watch lists although I knew people who were so I was fairly tight. Still I couldn't help thinking about the whole thing. It felt like having your neck in a guillotine with the rope securely tied off but noticing it beginning to unravel in the middle.

I was going back and forth between confidence and collapse when I got a call from my brother. I hadn't talked to him in over a month and I sure as hell hadn't told him about this. I didn't want to worry him but more importantly I didn't need the feds trying to drag him into it as a witness or anything else. He had a good life that he had worked very hard to get and I wasn't going to let anybody take that away from him or his family. As it turned out that choice was not going to be left up to me. My cancer is back he said, like a man very much resigned to his fate. Oh my God, no, not Diamo, not now! I listened as he explained his prognosis and it wasn't good. As he went on I felt my whole life beginning to crash. I could deal with the law. I could protect my wife and put her back in Sicily or someplace where they couldn't find her, but I quickly realized I was helpless against my brother's fate. I challenged him to seek other opinions, to go to Europe, hell drink monkey piss if you have to, but don't give up. He was calm in the face of it all as he explained that he had thoroughly researched everything I had just asked, except monkey piss, that wasn't going to happen. The cancer was back and even if he went through the hell of chemo and radiation he had maybe six months at best. He had talked with his wife and they both agreed that quality of life was far more important at this point than quantity and he would rather spend his time with her and the kids, and die peacefully in his own home.

What about you, he asked, how are things? I said everything was fine and he said "bullshit Dominick," I could hear it in your voice the minute you picked up the phone. I tried to convince him that everything was cool and thought I was doing a good job, and then he asked me if I was really going to lie to a dying man? I paused as I said through a struggling voice, no, no I will not lie to you. I'm in trouble. Over the next half hour I laid everything out for him as much as I could without making him an accessory. I had heard in the past week that the feds now knew who I was and were trying to obtain a federal warrant for my arrest, but due to the fact that I lived in a different state then where the crime had occurred and the fact that the key witness was a convicted felon, they were having a very hard time getting one. When I finished for the first time in our lives we were both completely at a loss for words. He said he needed to think about what I had told him and I said no you don't. You have a wife and kids that are going to lose their husband and father. That's what you need to think about and nothing else. What happens to me is what happens to me. I made the problem and I will handle it. He said okay but I knew now he was the one lying. I told him I loved him and he told me the same and we hung up the phone but promised to talk that weekend.

When I called back in a few days Diamo actually seemed happy. I thought that maybe he had gotten another opinion or had learned of a new treatment. Then again maybe it was just the pain meds, whatever it was I didn't care. I was just happy to hear his voice and know that for now he was okay. I've talked to my wife, he said, and I've researched your situation. Did you know that because it was a federal officer and it occurred while on duty that you can be given the death penalty? I hadn't meant to kill the guy but I also knew that this didn't mean shit. A fed was dead and the government sure as hell would try there level best to make me join him. I replied that I did not know that but it is what it is. Like I told you before it's my problem and there's nothing you can do to change that. He laughed as he said and that's where you are wrong my brother. He explained that he had spoken with his wife who was a very successful attorney, and they had come up with a solution. This isn't Sicily and you can't pay somebody off to make this go away I said, so unless you know something about the legal system that I've never heard of there is nothing you can do, and believe me brother I cannot tell you how much it means to me that you are trying. He asked me if I remembered when we were kids how we would occasionally use our identical appearance to pull jokes on people? We were, after all, identical twins and although our builds were now slightly different and he wore a full beard for many years which I never had. I remembered some of the times we had our fun and I smiled to myself as I now fondly remembered our younger years. I told him that yes I did remember but what has that got to do with my situation? He was actually enthusiastic as he said "I'm going to take your place..."

Like hell you are! There was no fucking way I was doing this! He had just a small amount of time left with his wife and children and no matter what the reason I would not be the one to keep them from being at his bedside when he passed. Now it was Diamo's time to be tough. Look, he said, I've talked this over until the early hours of the morning with Kayla and we both agree that it's what we want to do. I have to die, you don't, and if I have any say in it you're not going to. Goddamn it Diamo I can't ask you to do this! Well, he said, that's the beauty of it, you're not the one asking, I am. Now I was completely confused. What are you asking me to do, and he said I am asking you my brother to please let me save your life. I could not speak as the tears poured out and my chest shook from the sobs inside of me. Just then Isis walked in and thinking something was wrong rushed to my side to console me. Now I had to tell her...

The next few days were pretty rough. She was shocked at the revelation of both my work and my current situation although, she eventually admitted that she always figured that I had some under the table business interests, she just didn't know what. I told her that I would have confided in her earlier but I was concerned for her pregnancy and the safety of the babies. She was so blown away by my brother's offer and agreed we should try and find another way. We could leave the country. She had family in Greece and I had mine in Sicily. The only problem, and we both agreed, was that the federal government would not let this rest and we would always have to wonder. Still we did not want to take any of my brother's remaining time from his family. Maybe we'd just have to take our chances with going someplace else. The next morning a taxi pulled up in front of our house and my brother and his wife got out. After plenty of hugs and tears they both took on a serious look as they explained that we simply had to accept their offer. Time was of the essence and none of us had any idea when a caravan of federal agents was going to pull into the driveway. Diamo and Kayla explained that they had made their peace with the whole situation and in the end agreed that if taking my place would save my life, that's what they wanted to do. He said my kids are going to lose me and there isn't anything we can do about it, but your kids haven't even met you yet and there is something I can do to see that they do. This is no longer your decision Dominick, so let's make a good dinner tonight, drink some really expensive wine, and tomorrow you guys pack your stuff and get the hell out of here.

I looked at Isis and back at my brother and his wife, and as I walked over to wrap my arms around them both, with tears streaming once more down my face I finally said okay.

―――――――――――――

Thirty

When they finally showed up it was actually just two government sedans and not a huge dramatic event like we had expected. They rang the door and when the man answered they said Dominick Fortunata? As the man nodded his head they showed him a warrant for his arrest and asked him to please turn around and put his hands behind his back. Some of the neighbors were staring from their driveways and one commented that it looked like he's lost a bunch of weight as they led the suspect to the waiting sedan. The police interviewed some of the nearby neighbors and although they all thought he had a girlfriend or fiancé, they had not seen her in weeks. The police just assumed she had dumped him or he her. It didn't really mater. They had their guy and that's all they cared about. The trial was fairly quick, with the defendant waiving both his preliminary hearing and his right to a jury trial. He offered to plead guilty to a lesser charge if one could be offered and the prosecutor smiled as he said there would be no plea bargain on this case. You killed a federal officer and we will be seeking the death penalty. It was explained to him that if having a trial by judge was in fact his choice he would, for all practical purposes, give up his ability to file an appeal. He agreed that he understood and the trial soon began. The witness identified him and the defense did not really cross examine much. The man had explained to his attorney that he wanted it done quickly, and that's just what he got. The judge found him guilty and sentenced him to die by lethal injection. It would take at least three years to impose the sentence, but the prisoner was not going to last even three months.

With in a few weeks of his imprisonment he requested to go to the infirmary where after a battery of tests it was discovered that he had cancer. He was now confined to bed rest and given an ample supply of morphine to manage the pain. He kept his medication at the minimum to not cloud his mind as he liked to read and listen to music. He was sitting in a wheel chair looking out the window at the songbirds as his mind drifted back to the days in Floridia. He reflected on all of the things he and Dominick had done in their lives in spite of their circumstances. He kept a tiny ember of private satisfaction inside himself knowing that because of his gift, his brother would carry on. He missed his wife and his children and they had talked about letting them visit him in prison under the guise of being other family members. They agreed that it was better for the children to be told that he had passed away and not have to witness either the ravages of the cancer or the bars that now confined him. He had done well for himself and his wife would never have to work again if she chose but he knew this would never be the case. She would take some time off to mourn but like him she couldn't sit still for very long. He had asked her to make a promise before he left. Cry as much as you have to. Mourn for as long as you need to but allow yourself to be open to falling in love again. She said that although she truly wanted to give him the peace of answering yes, inside she had always known that he was the one and only man she would ever love. He understood and as they both embraced each other for the last time he looked into her tears filled eyes and said at least try. You can do that, I know you can. No promises, but at least try... She said she would and that was enough.

The last thing he heard in this world was the cheerful chirping of a beautiful red cardinal as his head came to rest on his chest, and he breathed no more. When the body was prepped for transfer to the family funeral home the doctor noticed a single bird tattoo on the upper left chest, and no other identifying marks.

Epilogue

We had booked a transatlantic cruise from New York to England and were half way across when the whole thing really hit me. Flying was out of the question as this whole thing had not yet panned out and as it happened I needed the time to think anyway. I was able to join Isis for meals but most of my other time I spent either in the cabin looking out at the ocean, or on the warmer days sitting in a topside chaise lounge analyzing my entire life. I couldn't relieve my guilt. If I hadn't chosen the profession I had, my brother would have at least been able to hold his wife's hand when he dies. My decisions had robbed them both of that and I couldn't shake it. I was now Diamo and had the passport and American driver's license to prove it. My wife was able to keep her identity and my brother's body would eventually be shipped across the Atlantic to be buried in our family plot. I dreaded the day of the funeral long before it ever came. I didn't know how I could look his wife in the eye with us both knowing what I had taken from her. I now carried a weight inside of me that seemed as if it would never leave.

We docked in England and after a couple days of rest boarded the ferry across the channel as we began to make our way back to Sicily. We traveled south through France and the wine country and my wife marveled at how beautiful it all was. When we stopped to eat she was equally enamored by the French cooking and the cozy chateaus that house the family-owned restaurants. For me the scenery all looked like a bad charcoal drawing and what food I did take lingered on my taste buds like ash. Still I kept up appearances and smiled falsely at the wonder of the southern French countryside. We drove across through Monaco and into northern Italy as she looked over at me, grabbing my hand reassuringly, and said that I was back where I belonged at last. I was Sicilian, not Italian, and there is a difference, but the last thing I wanted was a fight and I just smiled and nodded my head. We boarded another ferry that would take us to my homeland and for the first time in weeks I allowed myself just a glimmer of happiness. When we docked my father was waiting with some of his men and insisted on taking us to a local ristorante owned by one of his long time friends. I hugged him tightly and as we separated he still held me by both arms as he looked me in the eyes and said, it's okay Dominick, your brother loved you. I nodded but it still wasn't okay. I didn't know how long I would feel this way but I realized that I wasn't the only person mourning his loss so I kept it to myself. On the drive home my father handed me a small rectangular package that was addressed to him but was labeled care of Dominick Fortunata. It would be many weeks before I could reveal its contents. I didn't know who it was from and I thought it possible to be from Diamo but I needed to sort my mind out before I added anything else to the mix, so the package would sit unopened on my bedside dresser until I could open it.

Isis had the babies soon after and we named them Angel Marie and Diamo Dmitri in tribute to her father and my brother. The birth of our children forced me to take my mind off from my own issues and I was grateful for that. Isis would breast feed them and rest on the sunny veranda of the villa where I had first spoken with the Don many years ago. I helped my father with some of his affairs and we tended the cemetery in solemn preparation for the arrival of my brother's body. One day as we were working on mother's grave he stopped and looked at me as he asked me why my heart was so heavy? As he began to pull the weeds again it was much like when I lost Angelia. I had so many thoughts bottles up inside, my words and my tears flowed without stopping . When I had finished he motioned me to sit with him on the wooden bench. He reached into a basket that my mother had owned and pulled out two small wine glasses and a bottle of wine from his orchards. As he handed me a glass he began to speak; Dominick I knew you and your brother first as business men and then as my sons. I have known many people and ordered the deaths of many as well, and there is one thing I accept in this life. We live and we die, without exception. Your brother had cancer and nothing you could say or do would change that. Yes, but he could have died with his wife by his side instead of in some prison bed I said. Please, as he held up his hand to silence my words. Your brother loved you, and he was a grown man who not only greatly pondered his decision before offering it but also consulted his wife. Knowing that he did this I have even greater respect for Diamo than I already possessed. Although my heart will ache for a long time, I am very proud of him as a man, a husband, a son, and a brother. He knew that he would die, but he also knew that the one person who had looked out for him all of his life would die as well, but he had a way to prevent it. He spoke further and although I greatly loved my father for trying, it was a pain that I would simply have to bear. My father was the wisest man I have ever known and once again sensing the subtle defiance of his words, turned to me and took my forearm with a strength that I thought had long been lost. Dominick let me ask you one question and then I will never broach the subject again if this is your wish. I nodded my head as I looked at the ground. "Would you have done the same for Diamo if the positions had been reversed?"

I paused as I pondered the question and then with one hundred percent conviction, and yet another tear, said yes, of course I would. I would have done anything to help him. I know that, and so did he. So go ahead and miss him, cry more tears when you must, but please forgive yourself and understand that you allowed his death to not be in vain. You both gave each other a gift in the end that will last for eternity. For the first time in months the weight was gone. Although I greatly missed him, I now knew that our father was right and as he had said before, life must go on. Diamo's wife arrived the following month with my brother's body and we had a private service for him at our home, just like we had for our mother. I spent many hours sitting by his casket, asking myself still more questions and thinking back to our days as children. We buried him the next morning, and just before we closed the casket first my father, then me, and finally his wife, all bent to kiss him on the forehead one last time. I don't know why but as I gazed down at him for a moment it didn't look like my brother. I assumed the cancer was responsible for the obvious weight loss, but there was something else. I could have sworn he had tiny faded scars on his cheeks, jaw line, and around his eyes, but once again I considered the circumstances and assumed my mind and my emotions were just playing tricks on me.

I wanted to do something in memoriam and Kayla suggested a donation to the orphanage. With my father's assistance we purchased property right beside La Cassa Del Benefenicia and planted an orchard with peaches, apples, plumbs, oranges and lemons. The property would be operated by a trust so that it would only be used to help the kids and no one else. The children would have a supply of fresh fruit almost year round and would never have to steal it like we had.

Kayla stayed in Sicily for a month and it made my heart warm to see her children enjoyed the beauty and bounty as my brother and I had so long ago. One afternoon she asked me what I would do now. Lately, I had thought of this often. Sean had grown quite prosperous and could probably provide plenty of jobs in Ireland, his friend Mr. Wolfe was now in Spain and was running one of the largest criminal organizations in the country. As I would come to learn, even my wife's family had some unusual business interests in Greece. If I wanted to get back into the trade I would never have to enter the U.S. again, but as I thought of my life I knew that I wanted to go in a different direction. I could always get back in the restaurant business and I thought maybe I would. People had always told me that with the things I had seen in my life and the stories I had heard that I should write a book. I still had the unopened package that Diamo had sent and when I finally opened it I found his journal, a letter, and a key to a safe deposit box. His letter was much like my conversation with our father and as I finished I smiled as I thought of all the things two orphans had seen and done in their lives, and began to think maybe I would write about that. Maybe...

---

www.ingramcontent.com/pod-product-compliance
Lightning Source LLC
Chambersburg PA
CBHW030030180626
46810CB00001B/296